Something
on the Wind

Also by Barbara Moore

THE FEVER CALLED LIVING
HARD ON THE ROAD

Something on the Wind

BARBARA MOORE

Doubleday & Company, Inc.
Garden City, New York
1978

ISBN: 0-385-13171-2
Library of Congress Catalog Card Number 77-80483

For Mother and John,
always friends to the animals

One

THE MOMENT a tiny gray verdin piped its danger signal, the old dog crouched low on the ground, mute and motionless. The verdin was the quickest of all the desert birds to see a hawk. The dog listened for the rush of heavy wings, but he could hear only the murmur of running water—that, and the perilous noise that his two mules were making, loudly champing grass over by the wagon, apparently oblivious of the danger. He tensed. He was responsible for the mules. If they and not he were the target, he would have to go to their protection.

The dog made no effort to spot the hawk himself. He was too nearsighted, and, besides, predators were often a long distance away when a verdin sounded the warning that other species had learned to recognize. The dog had first heard its *gee-gee-gee!* as an eight-week-old pup. Now, seventy pounds of aging muscle and matted shag, he presented no attraction to airborne hunters, nor did a pair of fourteen-hundred-pound mules, but the dog didn't know that.

He waited, making himself small. In the tall cottonwood trees and the understory of mesquite along the edge of the stream, all the thronging birdlife froze. Lizards turned to stone. The mules alone had failed to understand the warning. Then the verdin churred loudly, this time *tsee-seesee,* only a song, and the other birds came to life again—the sedate flycatcher quietly foraging atop a weedy stem and the gaudy tanager claiming possession of a cottonwood twig. The hawk's distant passage was forgotten. The dog forgot it too, as well as the fancied danger to the mules, and resumed his investigation of their new home.

Home for the dog meant basically a man, the two mules, and a wagon, unchanging talismans in surroundings that changed constantly. Since the previous evening, they had been in a winding canyon high in the foothills of the dry Mazatzal Mountains in Arizona Territory, but the dog knew nothing of place names. He knew that a half-mile upstream a female antelope had paused to drink during the night. He knew that a ground squirrel stirred incautiously in a pocket of box elder fifty feet up a wash. He knew a grasshopper was climbing a blade of bunch grass in back of him. The dog knew everything he could smell and hear, taste and feel, and he found it richly sufficient.

He also knew that they would be stopping for the day instead of moving on. For one thing, the man had hobbled the mules and turned them loose to graze near a tumble of great boulders. Then, since breakfast, the man had occupied himself in the closed square at the back of the wagon, which made everything abundantly clear. The morning had dawned hot but glorious. Even though the dog wasn't especially hungry, thanks to a skilletful of biscuits sopped in bacon grease, he suddenly thought of going hunting. His floppy ears lowered and his stern sagged slightly, and he looked guiltily over his shoulder toward the wagon.

Leaving his charges all alone and unprotected was something the dog wasn't supposed to do. There were other rules. He had learned these, little by little, since he was a young dog still uncertain which new actions would bring punishment. But the dog had never gotten over the temptation to absent himself occasionally on private errands. And it wasn't as if the man had told him, "Stay," or said, "No," or tied him to the wagon, as he sometimes incomprehensibly did. The dog glanced up the streamlet that dropped from mirrored pool to pool descending the canyon, and he yawned nervously, considering crime. In mid-yawn, he started at a sudden sound. The man was coming out of the wagon. Now the man was walking toward him. Caught, already. His ears and stern drooped still further.

A reek preceded the man. It was pyrogallic acid and potassium cyanide, pyroxylin and alcohol, nitrate of silver and potassium iodide, all mixed together in a stench to rival a skunk's. The man was one of the West's traveling photographers, who, with glass plates and crude cameras, pursued with equal enthusiasm the squalor and splendor of the fading frontier. The smell of the chemicals he used always clung to his clothing, and the wagon was hopelessly permeated with it, and the bright, clean air of the morning received so strong a dose wafting from the wooden darkroom built on the back of the wagon that the dog sneezed and wiped at his nose with an oversized paw. The man stopped beside the dog to fill a water bucket in the stream and patted him absent-mindedly on the head. The dog was habitually given to a grave friendliness toward this man rather than to fawning enthusiasm. He didn't normally respond to patting with more than a polite wag, or, at most, a chin rested gently on the man's knee, but he took the pat for a sign of forgiveness and wagged his bobbed-off tail vigorously.

"Going to take a view of that biggest saguaro," the man told the dog in a cheerful but distracted sputter. He nodded toward a towering cactus, then raised speculative eyes to an enormous block of eroded rock above the boulders where the mules were grazing. "Bet if I could get up high somewhere, I could get a view of it reflected in the stream. Now wouldn't that be pretty?"

The dog listened attentively to the rush of sound. His understanding of human speech was largely limited to commands and a few pertinent nouns such as "skillet" and "dinner," and he caught only one word he knew, "view." "View" was complicated. Sometimes it meant paper things, but sometimes it meant the heavy camera the man carried about, and the man would close himself lengthily into the square at the back of the

3

wagon while fresh fumes of chemicals rose from unstoppered flasks. Temptation was getting a helping hand.

The man patted the dog again and rose with his bucket, and a new idea came to the dog. Could that pat be a sign of permission to go hunting? The dog cocked his head and opened his eyes wide, asking, but the man only whistled his way back to the wagon. That wasn't surprising. The man and mules both seemed to the dog highly illogical creatures at best, and of the two, the mysterious mules were far easier to understand.

But there was really nothing here at the camp that demanded the dog's attention. He examined a two-rut wagon road just in sight down the canyon for any signs of movement. All was quiet. All seemed well. The only reasonable thing to do was to track up the streamlet a few yards, just to investigate that tiny rustle in the sand, just to sniff around the roots of a mesquite tree, just lazily to pick up and sort the odors of . . .

Fresh jackrabbit! The old dog put his nose to the ground and his bobtail in the air, forgetting all else, and bounded up the canyon.

Later in the morning, when the photographer had climbed the cliff and fallen to the rocks below, something brushed the dog's consciousness, but he wasn't sure what it was. The dog hesitated, cataloging. Sandy soil, hot, pressing between toes. Cholla cactus ahead, almost hidden by a tall carpet of grass that had sprung up after the beginnings of the midsummer rains. The dog would steer well around it. He'd long since learned the lesson of cactus spines. Hours-old scent of mouse. Scent of elf owl, sleeping. Scent of lizard and tiny sound of same as it scurried from the shade of one bush to the next, tail up to escape the growing heat of the ground. Then came delicious scent of well-ripened cow manure on the wind. Delightful to roll in. He continued up the canyon instead of returning to the man, the mules, and the wagon.

Far downstream, the two mules, Old Jeb and Young Jeb, were napping, but they also opened great, liquid eyes and

4

looked around as if they'd heard something. They became restless. They made no attempt to climb the rocks where the man lay unconscious, but they did hop and shuffle in their hobbles as far as the two-rut wagon road. Then Old Jeb, the leader, noticed an easy approach to water where the ruts forded the stream, and they quieted, both enjoying a long, deep drink.

The mules were still at the ford when a German farmer drove by in a cart. New to a land where cactus grew more readily than the wheat and vegetables he was attempting to raise under irrigation, the farmer was not too new to know that mules were valuable property, and these two bright, cherry-red bays were surely aristocrats in the mule kingdom. The farmer was an honest man, but not everyone was. Why were the mules unguarded? He stopped to investigate. While he was looking in puzzlement at the big, blue, oddly shaped wagon, his own dog, a natural tracker, found the injured man in the rocks.

Knowing something of the dangers of moving an accident victim, the farmer left the man where he lay. Even more reluctantly, he left the mules. He was en route to a settlement named Amyville with a brimming cartload of carrots and sweet corn, and he worried that his vegetables would dry out if he didn't keep moving. But as soon as he had delivered the vegetables to the Cosmopolitan Restaurant in Amyville, he would go by the doctor's office to send help back to the man.

Dr. Harold J. DeMeyers already had a small crowd in his combination office, waiting room, and surgery. He was examining the settlement's leading livestock dealer, Z. Z. Gitz, for a liver complaint, and two women were waiting, meanwhile watching openly while he thumped Gitz's liver. Dr. DeMeyers was not a well man himself, nor was he happy, and he was exasperated when the farmer clomped in and, without even waiting his turn, began to declaim something more in

5

German than in English. Dr. DeMeyers interrupted him: "I said you will have to wait. Please take a seat."

The farmer tried again, and one of the women, Mrs. Costello, became interested. "He's saying something about a photographer. Why, that must be the photographic artist who was through town yesterday. He's hurt? The young man's hurt?"

The farmer nodded energetically, and the other woman, Mrs. Evans, chimed in. A photographer's wagon coming to town caused as much excitement as a minstrel show's band wagon, and most of Amyville's citizenry had turned out to see it. "Would you believe it?" she said. "I almost sat to the poor man for my portrait, but he charged a whole dollar. Mr. Gitz, I saw you there. My husband said you were trying to talk the young man into selling his mules."

Z. Z. Gitz turned to her and said, "No'm, Mrs. Evans, I just sat for my portrait. Do any of you speak any German? Reckon the fellow's been robbed? Reckon he's dead?"

The whole business was very upsetting for Dr. DeMeyers. His patients kept gabbling at the farmer, and when they thought they had figured out the circumstances, they became increasingly excited. They made it obvious that they expected him to delay no longer than it took to complete their own treatments, then saddle his horse and grab his saddlebag and rush off to the injured man's assistance. His patients' expectations were of unusual importance just then. A drummer selling Samaritan Nervine had convinced the populace that it would cure everything from female weakness to epileptic fits, and these were the first patients he had seen in days. But he didn't want to go dashing off in the heat. Why, the dust alone would kill him.

"I'll tell you what, Doc. I'll drive you out to the canyon myself in my buckboard," Z. Z. Gitz unexpectedly offered. "Since this kraut didn't bring the poor fellow in, I guess we got no choice."

The German farmer did understand enough English to know he was being insulted. He had planned to accompany

6

the rescue party on the hot, dusty journey out to the canyon, but instead he stayed behind in Amyville. Dr. DeMeyers and Z. Z. Gitz had the dust all to themselves.

Once they reached the canyon, Z. Z. made his motive clear. He went instantly to look at the mules, not the man, and left Dr. DeMeyers to contend with the unconscious photographer. DeMeyers examined him. There was no way to get the injured man to the buckboard without help. He'd have to conduct his examination on the spot. But hurry. No telling how long the man had been lying there baking in the sun. The man was young. Definitely the photographic artist his patients had chattered about. A fifty-pound view camera lay in the fan of rocky debris near him. The man had obviously fallen off that big ledge of rock overhead while trying to climb up or down with that bulky camera over his shoulder, the fool. Possibly a concussion.

Heavy panting and scrabbling sounds told Dr. DeMeyers that Z. Z. Gitz was finally coming up to join him, but, having started, DeMeyers continued his examination. He promptly discovered at least one bone break, the left arm.

Z. Z. Gitz, on the other hand, seemed more interested in the young man's state of finances than in his health. He said, "Dressed kind of rough, wouldn't you say? I'll bet the poor fellow hasn't got a dollar in those denims, though I paid him one myself yesterday."

"I haven't gone through his pockets," DeMeyers said shortly.

"Of course not. But darned if I wouldn't if I was a hardworking doctor that had to worry about his fee. I'll tell you what I've been thinking, Doc. I can sell this poor fellow's mules for him, just a quiet, quick little auction out at my brother's place. Then he can pay for his treatment."

DeMeyers found the thought attractive but dangerous. "The man isn't dead," he said. "He's just unconscious. Besides, maybe he's got a pocketful of gold."

Z. Z. took a look at the man's pockets and pulled out only a

7

penknife and some change. "Some people just beat anything," he said. "It looks like he's already spent his takings, and yet the fellow's got a pair of mules that would sell easy for eighty, a hundred dollars each. Mule rich and purse poor, you might say."

DeMeyers motioned Z. Z. back and went on with his examination, but with a slightly different attitude. Fractured left arm above elbow, twenty dollars. Two fractured fingers on the left hand, three dollars each. Lacerated lip there, partly concealed by a neat mustache? No, fancy that, the young man had a harelip, apparently poorly stitched up in babyhood. DeMeyers could have done a better job than that at surgical repair. Well, all right, there was the probable concussion. Better yet, a fracture of the cranium. Trepanning and elevating a skull fracture, why, if it came to that, his bill might jump to well over a hundred dollars.

Of course, DeMeyers had never done a trepanation before, but he wasn't one of your frontier medicos who just set up shop with no training whatever; he had a real medical degree from the august University of Pennsylvania. He'd do his best for the injured man, but even at two hundred dollars for the mules, it looked as if the patient would end up in Dr. DeMeyers' debt once Z. Z. took what he was undoubtedly contemplating as his split. It would be an act of charity.

The injured man moaned, the first sound he'd made, and Z. Z. eyed him squeamishly. "He's not plugging out, is he, Doc?" he asked.

"No, his pulse is strong. But you'd better help me get him down to the buckboard. You take his feet. There's apparently nothing broken at that end."

"He's got some blankets and stuff in that wagon of his," Z. Z. said. "Let's pack him into my buckboard real careful. Seems to me we ought to swing cross-country to take the mules to my brother's place. It's not a bit rougher than this sorry excuse for a road, and it's faster, if you get what I mean."

The two men exchanged a long look. Staying off the road

8

would also mean the mules wouldn't be seen. Dr. DeMeyers withheld verbal agreement. But neither did he object when, leaving the canyon with his patient apparently riding comfortably in the bed of the buckboard and the two bright bay mules tugging behind, Z. Z. pulled off the wagon road after only a short distance and headed through the sprawling privacy of the desert.

Far up the canyon, the desert rested, awaiting the heat of the afternoon. As the dog flopped panting into an inch-deep pool, a white-winged dove in the tallest heights of the cottonwoods began calling his loud, obsessive question, *"Who* cooks for you?" Cicadas burred their metallic song. Two, or perhaps more, jackrabbits met near the streamlet not fifty yards up and crept under a bush to rest, the dog noted, but he'd hunted rabbit futilely all morning and now he was too worn out to do anything about it. The dog also rested in the shallow, shaded water. Thought, rarely more than a floating awareness for him, diffused still further. Time had no meaning. Hopes, aspirations, fears—none existed. The dog and all that surrounded him were one. After a while, he slept.

Paradise lasted until a zebratail lizard crawled to the edge of the old dog's pool to sip a few rare drops of water. The dog stirred and the lizard scampered away. Returned to full consciousness by the sound, the dog thought first not of rabbits but of the iron skillet in which he was fed. Failing fresh game —and his master was a poor shot who usually failed to provide it—the dog generally dined each evening on jerked beef softened with boiling water and left to sit until chewable by worn and blunted teeth. He was aware that it was too early for his dinner, but he was always an optimist about food. So, thinking jerked beef, the dog shook himself thoroughly and turned his steps homeward.

Because of the wagon's stench, the dog had to place no demands on his sensitive sense of smell to know when he was nearing "wagon," and at that first scent the guilty feeling re-

9

turned overwhelmingly. His pace didn't stop, but it slowed. The inevitable scolding awaited. Soon he picked up stale mule smell. There was man smell too, not only his master's, but a smell of strange men. That wasn't uncommon, nor was it uncommon to analyze and note the fading smell of strange horses. The dog was not suspicious of strangers. Humans and animals were always coming and going around his wagon, and the dog knew their presence had something to do with the reeking chemicals.

A strong odor of fresh chemicals should have greeted him as he neared their campsite, but didn't. His black nose quested. No smell of simmering stewpot, from which he could usually count on begging a helping. He also should be hearing a welcoming nicker from the hobbled mules, but there was nothing, no fresh scent, no sound, not even their shuffling step. The dog didn't feel worried, merely curious, and he broke from trot into easy lope, hurrying to find out what was going on.

He was reassured by the sight of the familiar wagon, parked where he had last seen it in the shade of the cottonwoods near the stream bed. The dog's skillet sat on the ground by a circle of cookstones. He checked it as a matter of form, but, as his nose had already told him, it now contained nothing but a few ants. The breakfast-blackened stones were warmed only by the sun, not fire. Where was the man? Where were the mules?

A ripple of anxiety washed over the old dog. It was quite one thing for him to sneak away from his charges, but another for them to go off on their private errands and leave him by himself. He whirled at an unexpected sound, then relaxed. It was just a cactus wren scolding from the safety of the big saguaro cactus, which had visibly begun to distend its wrinkled, century-old bulk with the tons of water it would store for the coming dry season.

Normally, the dog had no such anticipations of a future. He was absorbed in the moment, with only occasional recollections of a past and no thought at all of time's tomorrows.

10

Big, bobtailed, with oversized feet that gave him a clownish look, he had black-and-white fur that was beginning to thin, and he was turning gray on the muzzle. He often woke up in the mornings feeling stiff in the joints, but the bobbed tail still wagged politely upon each morning's first stirring by his master.

The man was not his first master, and he remembered that. The smell of licorice would bring back a moment's vivid sensation of jumping over a rain-filled ditch at the heels of a little boy. The smell of neat's-foot oil and saddle leather brought a more recent, troubling sense of another man, but the dog lacked the power of imagery and could recall him only fleetingly and imperfectly. The present was all.

For some time now the present had held this new man, source of food and friendly fingers scratching behind the flopping ears. Having little option, the dog had accepted the change. But from the beginning, the new man had seemed inseparably tied to the wagon and the mules and the skillet and the bedroll behind the wagon seat and the other accouterments of their wayfaring life that represented home and security to the dog.

There was another place, however. The man had taken the dog there only twice between trips, but twice had been enough to give it some feeling of home. There was a cabin. The wagon stopped rolling there and just sat. Behind the cabin was a field of wild hay where mice could be caught, and in front of it was a cold, fast-running stream, not a warm, trickling flow like that in the canyon. Most importantly, this place had a kitchen. It was the only kitchen the dog had ever been allowed to enter, and therefore it remained in his memory in the form of warmth from a stove, beside which the dog could lie to twitch and dream and to listen for the sound of a knife chopping. The dog could sit and wait while the knife chopped, and sometimes a miraculous tidbit fell on the floor. A chunk of fresh beef, a bit of celery, the peel of a carrot—the dog gobbled them all down.

11

So although he couldn't remember many things clearly, he remembered the kitchen, but he couldn't remember how long it had been since he last saw it. Besides, the kitchen was somewhere else, somewhere in the whole of the West throughout which his various masters' wanderings had taken him, from Texas to Colorado to California and back again, whereas the empty skillet and the wheels of the smelly wagon were right here beside him. Surely the man and the mules would return. The dog curled up under the wagon wheels to wait for them. Even yet he wasn't really worried. He resumed his interrupted nap.

But when distant thunder awoke the dog near sunset, he began to feel distinctly uneasy. Both his stomach and his brain had an excellent sense of time, when he cared to consult them, and surely he was being kept unduly long from his dinner. By now it had escaped his memory that he had earned a scolding, and he embarked upon an investigation.

The dog was an uncertain sheep dog mix, a natural herder rather than a really gifted tracker. Besides, the ground surface was dry. And it had been hot all day. And a light wind was blowing. It took much casting back and forth before the dog located a trail that led up into the boulders. As twilight fell he lingered on the rocks for a long while, snuffling about. The man's camera still lay there. The smell of man around it was clear, not only that of his own man but of the strangers and of a strange dog. Then they went . . . where? Impossible to tell.

Tracking was easier back in the grass around the wagon. Here scent of the visiting horses, there the scent of the strangers, over here in the crushed vegetation his own mules. They had been grazing near the cottonwoods, grazing, still grazing, and here, yes, here mule, horse, and man smells joined, all heading to the two-rut wagon road. A lingering hint that was mostly the characteristic scent of his man's clothing indicated that his own man and the others had gone off with the mules somewhere down that road.

The dog sat down and whined, staring in the direction the

12

tracks led. The blue haze of dusk was giving way to the vast, silent blackness of a land in which nothing moved but the feet and coils of the feeders-by-night, and nothing sounded but the dry whisper of the wind. It was a hard, wild land, its hostility affirmed by the very name humankind had given it. Mazatzal, "the empty place between," the Paiute Indians first called it. Prospectors and would-be settlers who succeeded them added Suicide Ridge and Deadman Creek, Hardscrabble Mesa and Lousy Gulch, Hells Hole, Poison Canyon, Bloody Basin. It was a bad place to be alone.

But in the deepening shadows of the cottonwoods there was still the wagon, under which the dog had trotted most days and curled up to sleep most nights. The wagon was one of his charges. Like the mules and the man, it both offered and required protection. He went back to it and reared up, mouth open, sniffing deeply to gauge its contents. The man's blanket roll was not behind the spring seat where it was always kept. But everything else seemed normal. The dog dropped down lightly and moved to the front of the wagon. There seemed nothing to do but go on waiting. He would crawl next to the wheels to sleep.

But where were the man and the mules? Overhead in the cottonwoods an owl hooted, three soft notes. The dog's head went up, and a low moan escaped his throat. He was an old dog and well mannered, and he quieted after that. But had the moan gone higher and louder, it would have become a long howl of loneliness.

Two

THE FIRST SOUND that awakened Dr. DeMeyers the next morning in the settlement was the slap-slap-slap of the woman across the alley making tortillas. First she made tortillas for her husband's breakfast, then for her teen-age sons, then for the younger children, and then she began making them all over again for the husband and sons to take for their lunch into the foothills, where they toiled in a small silver mine. If Dr. DeMeyers awoke before the woman, as he often did, he lay alternately coughing and gritting his teeth, waiting for the soft slapping to begin, like the sound of rain dripping off a roof. Soon the water carriers would begin their horrible screeching out front, "A-gua-a-a-a-a p-u-r-a-a-a-a"—pure water. The trailed a's always sounded to DeMeyers as if a massacre was taking place in the streets.

Of streets, Amyville had two. When Dr. DeMeyers first arrived from Philadelphia, seeking nature's cure for a consumption that had attacked his lungs, the settlement had had three streets. Then silver had dwindled in the mines and so had a row of booming saloons which had provided him a steady flow of patients in the form of stabbings, shootings, and poisonings both accidental and otherwise.

Amyville was dying. Dr. DeMeyers wished it dead. He wished he had never come to Arizona Territory, and he wished that he could leave. He told himself he would go instantly if he could only get a little money ahead. Money or no money, he thought every morning that today he might just ride away, but

15

he never did. Instead, he lay coughing until dust began to puff in clouds above the hoofs of the loose cows, wandering pigs, and the occasional white-tailed deer strayed down from the mountains that made up Amyville's main traffic. The dust blew across a vacant lot next door and through DeMeyers' open bedroom window. He would think of the partitioned-off pharmacy that he ran in conjunction with his practice and of the pills of one, two, and three grains of opium he made up every Saturday afternoon for the Saturday-night run of miners too poorly paid to patronize the settlement's remaining saloons. Finally he would get up and take a one-grain opium pill, swearing it would be the last he would ever take, and so begin his day.

Today, after the opium pill, it occurred to Dr. DeMeyers that he had a patient "hospitalized" on a cot in a small room across the hall from the kitchen. There would be no way to make coffee without the patient's seeing him and expecting attention. Dr. DeMeyers' daily burden of despair settled on him more heavily. He didn't feel up to the practice of medicine yet.

On the other hand, probably the patient was still unconscious. The man had managed nothing but groggy moans since they'd brought him in yesterday, minus two red mules. Trepanation for a skull fracture had seemed more likely by the hour.

This morning Dr. DeMeyers felt far more dubious about attempting to saw open a man's skull. He was almost relieved when he walked softly down the hall and saw the young man sitting on the edge of the cot, as if waiting patiently. But then DeMeyers remembered the mules Z. Z. Gitz had taken and felt a wave of apprehension.

"Tut," he clucked, "lie back down immediately. You're a sick man."

The man lay down obediently and smiled at DeMeyers. A pity about that deformation of the upper lip. He had pleasant features, otherwise, and a pair of magnificent, deep-hazel eyes, as open and innocent as a child's. "Mighty sorry," the patient

16

said shyly. It apparently required effort to say it, and De-Meyers became alert. A severe blow on the head could deaden certain nerve functions.

"How does your head feel?" DeMeyers asked cautiously.

"Pretty good. Just aching some." The man's gaze went to the cast on his arm. "I guess I got hurt, didn't I?"

"You fell."

"I sure do appreciate you looking after me. Sir, I'm sorry to be troubling you, but I guess I've just been sitting here worrying—old Nemo and the Jebs, they're all right, aren't they? I mean, I've got this old dog and a couple of mules. I guess somebody's looking after them too, isn't that right?"

DeMeyers flushed. "Yes, of course," he said.

The young man's trusting eyes beamed. "That sure is a relief," he said. "You know how it is. Animals, well, they depend on you."

DeMeyers tried to think not of mules but of medicine. The man's words still came out hesitantly, as if he had to wrestle a moment with them before they could be spoken. Head wound on the right side—the peculiarities of human anatomy were such that control could be impaired on the whole left side of the body. "Have you had any difficulty moving your left arm and leg?" he asked the patient.

"Why, how in the world did you know that?" the young man said. "They felt dead as could be when I woke up in the night, but then they got pins and needles after a while, and now I can move them pretty good."

"And your face? You have full feeling in the left side of your face? You're talking queerly."

The man's free hand crept to his mouth to hide it. "Oh," he mumbled, "well, that's nothing. I always talk that way."

The harelip, of course. DeMeyers felt stupid for mentioning it. "You should have a good surgeon take a look at that lip," he said, trying to sound brisk and professional. "Even if earlier repair has been imperfectly performed, there's an operation that can be done so excellently that any disfigure-

17

ment is hardly detectable. But, naturally, it costs money. Now—"

"Say, that's right," interrupted the patient eagerly. "I hope you've still got my boots somewhere around. There's a couple of twenty-dollar gold pieces under the right sole. I'll want to be paying you for my care. And for the animals too, of course. And if that's not enough, I've got a letter of credit from my bank up in Colorado tucked away safe in my wagon. Say, Doc, I guess somebody brought in my camera and my wagon too, didn't they?"

They had left them, the camera by accident and the wagon by design. Z. Z. Gitz hadn't thought anybody in his right mind would buy an ungainly blue contrivance with a sort of tall, enclosed box at the rear where the photographer presumably developed his plates. Then, too, the wagon was painted in neat gold paint proclaiming, "Calvin Fairchild, Photo. Artist," and, on the other side, "Views! Portraits!! Stereoptic Views!!!"

At the thought that this Calvin Fairchild, Photo. Artist, was actually solvent, Dr. DeMeyers flushed a deeper red. "Shh," he said. "Don't talk so much. You've got to rest."

"Whatever you say. But, Doc, if they haven't brought in my wagon yet, I'd surely be much obliged if—"

"Don't worry about it. Rest."

"I'd be mighty glad to pay somebody for—"

"Yes, yes. Not another word now, Mr. . . . Fairchild? If you can't follow my instructions, I can't be responsible for you."

The patient subsided. But he looked so worried that Dr. DeMeyers felt a pang of sympathy. He assured him he would have Mr. Woodruff at the livery stable send out for the wagon that very morning.

Fetching in the ridiculous wagon and having somebody whistle up the old dog his patient was so worried about was the least he could do, Dr. DeMeyers thought miserably as he went into the pharmacy a few minutes later and stood staring at the big glass bottle that held the one-grain opium pills. Ap-

18

parently the man might not even have a concussion, just a residue of mild dizziness and brief recurrences of double vision from the crack he took to the head, although one would have to keep him quiet and observe him for a few days to be sure. That left one fractured arm above elbow and two fractured fingers, total twenty-six dollars. And Z. Z. Gitz was not a man to relinquish two hundred dollars' worth of mules without an argument.

What to do about those mules? He'd have to try to get a message to Z. Z., but it might already be too late. DeMeyers averted his eyes from the bottle of opium pills and tried to think. He found it easier to think of the dog. Mules were just transportation, but a dog could be an intimate companion. Funny there had been no dog around when they brought in the young man yesterday. It would be a pity if it strayed off. There were coyote packs and wolves and plenty of cougars in these mountains. Maybe he would even ride out to the canyon with the livery-stable boy and bring the dog in himself. That way he could delay a little longer in informing his patient that he was no longer the owner of a pair of fine red mules.

In the canyon, the desert celebrated the simple fact of being alive. Rejuvenated by the summer rains and the cool of the morning, new-minted poppies flaunted their golden banners. In the rocks above the wagon, the dry, thorny wands of the ocotillo bushes sported tiny new leaves of an acid green. The cactus wren in the biggest saguaro was wide awake and had been scolding at the recumbent form of the dog since first light.

There were not even ants this morning in the dog's skillet. His hunger was sharp by now. His impulse was to go on waiting patiently right where he was, guarding the familiar objects, but the hunger kept bringing him to his feet to recheck yesterday's scent of mules in the grass and faint scent of man leading to the rutted road. The morning was still. Due to a cloud cover, it was cooler than yesterday. Though the scent clinging to the absorbent grass was nearly twenty-four hours older, it was intensified by a touch of moisture in the air. Lying under the wagon, the dog gazed again and again in the direction the mule tracks led.

He didn't reason out a decision. He simply made it. Suddenly he stood and trotted off toward the wagon road, trailing the man and the mules.

At midmorning, when the fourteen-year-old livery-stable boy arrived with a team of horses to fetch the traveling photographer's wagon and look for some old dog, the dog was long gone.

Three

MOST PEOPLE believed that in following a trail a dog went along picking up the scent of footprints, but old Nemo followed a whole channel of airborne scent molecules that his mules had pumped out like bellows to linger in their wake. It was a complex chemical process, but as far as Nemo was concerned, he simply sniffed. This drew the molecules into the back of his nostrils, where they passed instantaneously over a labyrinth of odor-detecting cells, flashing a message to the brain: his mules.

If the dog could pick up odors better than a human, it was only because he had more olfactory cells, and he applied them with particular enthusiasm to such things as a pile of yesterday's mule droppings. Few humans would have cared for the dog's job, but, then, although the dog could smell the timid perfume of desert flowers as he passed them by, he had no interest whatever in flowers and far preferred animal droppings. But trailing was a tough, tedious job. Although the dog covered only six or seven roundabout miles, the cloud cover was burning off and the temperature was shooting past ninety by the time he fetched up at a sun-bleached, two-story frame building with the sign, "Gitz Hot Springs Hotel, a Christian Home for the Weary."

The hotel stood in total isolation at the base of a butte two miles south of Amyville. First fruit of a land and improvement company, it was also the last. Its proposed croquet lawns, tenpin alleys, and billiard parlors never materialized. It did have a smelly hot spring and an assortment of wooden bathhouses,

21

and, dating from the ownership of L. L. Gitz, brother to Z. Z. Gitz, a corral and sundry adobe outbuildings to serve as barn and storerooms. All were crumbling. While the original promoters had circularized the East with brochures aimed at fanciers of therapeutic travel in a pure atmosphere, they failed to raise enough funds for the railway line they also hoped to build, and the hotel was too difficult of access. A few dedicated health seekers managed to track it down, but none ever returned for a second visit. Why bother? The Montezuma Hot Springs Hotel in New Mexico had waters so cosmetic in their action that all ladies departed with velvety complexions. At the new Hotel Raymond in California one could pass the time listening to its author-in-residence deliver lectures on natural history. Or, if one believed those theories about germs or bacteria or whatever, everyone knew the buggy things couldn't live at an altitude above five thousand feet, so ho for Colorado Springs and the cushioned comfort of the Antlers Hotel.

L. L. Gitz bought the building with an eye to turning it into a miner's boardinghouse, and it was a sore trial when the mines began to close. He currently did a brisker business selling fodder than he did a night's lodging. Although it went against his principles, L. L. also sold tobacco and whiskey. Even a good Christian had to live, he rationalized. Mrs. Gitz, however, found the whiskey a personal temptation. When she was sober, she provided the meals served in the dining hall, aided by their twelve-year-old daughter.

The aroma of frying steak was in the air, and the old dog put up his nose and snuffled greedily. The faint chemical smell of his man's clothing seemed to have disappeared, but the mule scent went beside the barn, and he trotted after it. Hens squawked, alarmed. The dog hesitated. Chickens.

He began to tremble, ears cocked, nostrils flaring. After a full day's fasting, he was very hungry. But chickens . . . chickens . . . fluttering . . . frantically running . . . Chasing chickens was on his list of forbidden activities, and to kill and eat one . . . The only crime worse than killing chickens, he had painfully learned as a pup, was stealing and eating human's food. Such food had to be given.

The dog trembled harder, but he moved on. So he was bewildered to hear a voice call, "Bad dawg! You bad, bad dawg!"

It was a dirty woman in a dirty apron, come to see what had disturbed the hens. The dog's ears and stern automatically lowered at the sound of "bad," and he cowered. The woman came closer, and the dog retracted his lips to expose his teeth in a grimace. Then his bobtail wagged. The ferocious look was a canine grin.

On the heels of the woman came her immature counterpart, a dirty girl in a smaller, dirtier apron, carrying a broom. She ran at the dog and thrust the broom in his face. He lurched away as the woman cried, "Don't hit him. He wasn't doing nothing."

Tight-lipped, the girl said, "If he got one of them hens—"

"No, Tilda, he was just walking by. Not a hen's lost a feather. He's had good training somewhere. That's the kind of dawg you ought to have, if you was ever to want a dawg."

The girl gave her mother a disapproving look. "Poppa don't like no dawgs. Dawgs is just extra work."

"Well, he looks hungry, poor old thing," the woman said.

"Old is right," the girl said. "Somebody ought to shoot him and put him out of his misery."

"That dawg's not miserable. He's happy. See, he's wagging his tail."

"I'm gonna go get Poppa."

"Don't you dare!"

"I'm gonna."

The woman grabbed the broom from the girl. "I'm only going to get that dawg something to eat," she said. "You don't go telling your poppa, and I'll give you the little scissors my momma give me. They're real silver."

"Don't want no scissors."

"Then what do you want?"

"I want the coral necklace you got hid in your old dresser trunk."

The mother's strained, weary face relaxed into a shadow of an amused smile. "All right. But your poppa'll never let you wear it. Vanity is sin."

"So's wasting good food on a mangy dawg," the girl said. "The Lord put animals on this earth for people to live on, not the other way around."

"That's enough, now. You run peek at the corral and make sure your poppa's still busy. I'll go bring something for the dawg."

"Don't you go giving that old dawg more than one piece of that meat."

"I won't," the woman said. She kept her word, but, in the fly-filled kitchen with the dog waiting hopefully outside the door, she chose the largest piece of steak from a plate that had cooled enough for the flies to start landing, then grabbed four biscuits, and, not content, she risked adding a fried apple pie. She put her offerings on the back step. Careless of splinters, the dog gulped the food down, then licked the wood and paced a few steps, looking for something else.

The woman studied him. "Water," she finally decided. "That's what you want. You're thirsty." There was a water bucket in the kitchen, half-full, and she scooted it out the door. The water was from the spring. It was yellowish red and tasted the way it looked, like rusted iron. But the dog was hot and thirsty. He drank the whole half bucket and would cheerfully have drunk more. He drank so much that his stomach ballooned noticeably.

The girl came running, fast, from the direction of the corral. Laughing, the woman called to her, "Listen, Tilda, he drunk so much water he's sloshing."

"Git rid of that dawg," the girl panted. "Poppa's coming."

"Oh!" the woman said. "Oh, dawg, you got to git!"

She danced up and down frantically. The dog knew what "git" meant, but only when it was said in the proper tone. He moved back a pace and sat down and stared expectantly at his new friend.

"Mercy me," the woman said, and she picked up the broom and hit him squarely on the head.

The dog yelped in fear and in pain. He tumbled backward, then regained his balance. He wagged his tail tentatively, ready to forget what might have been just an accident, like getting a paw stepped on, and started to sit down again. The woman began to cry. She rushed him with the broom.

"Git, dawg." She swatted. "Oh, Lord, I'm sorry. Now you git." She swatted. "You hear me? You git."

The tone of voice was right this time, and the intent of the broom was unmistakable. Bobtail tucked tight to his rump, the dog fled around the corner of the bathhouses, just as L. L. Gitz came around the corner of the barn. The man stared suspiciously at the girl and the weeping woman. "What's going on here?" he demanded.

"Nothing," the woman mumbled.

The girl piped up. "Nothing but Momma burned her finger frying the steak."

The woman nodded, and L. L. shrugged. He fished a key from his pocket and told the girl, "Go get me a bottle." The sale ain't going so good. Your Uncle Z. Z. says we got to loosen 'em up." To the woman he added, "Stop that sniffling now. A little burn, that don't hurt much."

The woman succeeded in stifling her tears by the time her daughter stepped to the kitchen door to hand out the requested bottle. "You be bringing them up for dinner soon?" the daughter asked.

"I'll be bringing 'em up when I'm ready," Gitz said. He frowned and looked at the girl's dirty face and the woman's teary one, then shrugged again and trudged off. The woman sat on the splintery steps and stared at the grease spot where the dog had eaten.

"I reckon that old dawg thinks we hate him," the girl said.

The woman roused herself. "No, he doesn't," she said. "That was a smart old dawg. He just ran away because he was startled. I didn't hit him hard. And so he ran off, and he's sitting down somewhere and he's figuring out, 'Oh, now I see. That man was coming, and he don't like no animals except to work 'em to death, but that sure was a nice lady and a nice little girl, and that sure was a fine dinner they give me.'"

The girl stared at her mother, then she laughed. "That's silly. Now get up from there, or your beans'll be burning. You can get me my coral necklace now. And you made me tell a lie to my poppa, so I guess I'll just take those real silver scissors too."

Four

THE WOMAN was mistaken in her assessment of the dog's powers of understanding. Offended and scared, the dog slunk inside one of the open bathhouses and lay panting in back of a vast wooden tub. He could hear the voices of men down a slope by the corral, but his master didn't seem to be among them. Even though a little breeze brought a strong scent of his mules, he feared to approach. An unprovoked broom attack had shaken his confidence.

He waited, caught between fear and the desire to go to the mules, while by the corral Z. Z. Gitz took the bottle from his brother and said to Solomon Wickersham, "Wet your throat, Mr. Wickersham. Could be we got some talking to do."

Mr. Wickersham—forwarding and commission merchant, freights promptly forwarded to Solomonville, Safford, Pima, Camp Thomas, San Carlos, Globe, Tucson, Phoenix, and all points in southern Arizona and western New Mexico—was from Amyville and was not unfamiliar with L. L. Gitz's brew. He declined and the bottle passed to William Atkins of Tempe—carpenter, cabinetmaker, and furniture dealer, coffins and undertaking a specialty. Undertaker Atkins accepted, staring over the bottle at the two mules in the dusty corral, which otherwise held three gaunt horses and an elderly burro with haunted eyes. One of the mules stood aloofly in the patterned shade of a shed roofed only by ocotillo branches flung over a rough frame. The mule stared directly at the men, as haughty as an Englishman staring at an unwelcome stranger. The other

27

mule nervously danced in the corral, flashing from one end to the other. His red hide gleamed in the sunshine, and Undertaker Atkins said, as if for the dozenth time, "But I tell you, Mr. Gitz, for a proper funeral you need *horses,* and they got to be *black.*"

"I expect you're right," said Z. Z. mildly. "Of course, some folks would feel mighty proud to be carried off to the graveyard by blue-blooded nobility, but maybe folks in Tempe don't care about such things."

"Nobility? I'd sure like to hear just what's noble about bay mules in a funeral procession."

"Oh, did I forget to mention it?" Z. Z. directed his words to Mr. Atkins, but his eyes kept wandering to Mr. Wickersham. "Both those mules are direct descendants of Compound."

Undertaker Atkins looked questioningly at Mr. Wickersham and the stolid, silent brother. "Who's Compound?"

"You sending me up?" asked Z. Z. "You can't mean to tell me you never heard of George Washington's very own donkey. Next thing, you'll be telling me you never heard that George Washington was the father of mule breeding."

"I guess I thought he was the father of the country."

"Well, sir, he sure was the father of Compound, in a manner of speaking."

"You telling me the truth?"

"If I'm not, I'll eat my shoe buttons. Now, mind, I'm not telling you being descended from any old George Washington donkey is all that unique. He used to offer them around for stud, improving the breed, and the finest jack stock in this country can be traced back to the animals he produced. But Compound. To come down straight from Compound. Well, I guess that is unique."

Undertaker Atkins, who sipped steadily at Gitz's brew, apparently not minding its flavor, looked dazzled. "Doggone it, if they just weren't red," he said.

Mr. Wickersham spoke up. "The one that's acting up—he's a little young, isn't he?"

28

"A broken five-year-old. Perfect age."

"I'd have said more like a four-year-old."

"Hmm, hmm," said Z. Z. "Seems I've noticed you've always been more a Mexican mule man than a U.S. mule man, Mr. Wickersham. Might know where I could get you twenty or thirty Mexican mules dirt cheap. U.S. mules just might fit better with Mr. Atkins' needs. Take that other mule there, he's just rising seven. Give a powerful mule like that good care, he'll still be rendering faithful service twenty-five years from now. Your horse, he's an old-timer at fifteen."

"Yes," said Undertaker Atkins, "but I just don't know if I could rise to a hundred twenty-five dollars a head, seeing as they're red. For a proper funeral procession, even a President George Washington mule got to be black."

"I expect you're absolutely right. Of course, a man could always dress 'em fancy in a two-piece black running suit, and put a fine black plume on those showy heads carried so high, but those well-pointed ears sticking out and those trim, shapely legs stepping so dainty and dignified to the graveyard for the next twenty-five years would still be red. Gentlemen, I'll bet my sister-in-law's good dinner is getting cold waiting for us. What say we all go have a bite?"

No one moved except Z. Z.'s brother, and after two steps he turned and came back to the corral, looking sheepish. Silence fell.

After a long pause, Mr. Wickersham said, "Mule dealer up in Globe, he's offering fine Texas mules for seventy-five dollars a head."

"Oh, well, a *Texas* mule," Z. Z. sighed.

"Maybe he said New Mexico mules," Mr. Wickersham said, sounding slightly defensive.

The two men regarded each other quietly. Undertaker Atkins began to look agitated. "All right, I'll give you a hundred dollars a head for them," he said. "Seeing as they're red, there's not—"

"A hundred and ten," said Mr. Wickersham, showing serious interest for the first time.

"Now, wait," said Undertaker Atkins. "I mean, they're *red,* but I suppose I could go a hundred fifteen—"

"A hundred and twenty-five," said Mr. Wickersham.

"Hundred twenty-five dollars for some old mule?" said his opponent. "I don't care if they are George Washington mules, they're *red.*"

"Hundred twenty-five," repeated Mr. Wickersham. "That's my last offer, Mr. Atkins. Raise it, and they're yours."

"Well," mumbled Undertaker Atkins. "Well, all right then. A hundred twenty-six dollars. Good night, for red mules."

"Hundred thirty," said Mr. Wickersham promptly.

Undertaker Atkins' mouth dropped open and he looked outraged, but then his mouth snapped shut and he said nothing. He turned on his bootheel and started for the main building.

"Sold!" said Z. Z. Gitz. "Let's all go have that good dinner."

But Mr. Wickersham was familiar not only with the quality of the Gitz brew but of the Gitz cooking. He left within the quarter hour, the two mules on lead ropes behind his buggy.

Mr. Wickersham felt good. He liked to win, no matter what the prize, and he cocked his hat at a jaunty angle and whistled to himself as he left behind the rusty spring where the hotel promoters had dreamed of empire. En route to Amyville, he passed other dreams. To the left, a gaping prospect hole spoke of a would-be silver mine. Along the road a canal company had dreamed for a few years of digging a new, bigger irrigation canal atop the centuries-old remnants of one dug by prehistoric Indians to water their squash and beans. Everywhere stretched dry rangeland, overgrazed, the creosote bush and desert broom creeping in to replace the grasses, empire of a failed cattle company which was to have sold livestock and cured meats of all descriptions.

30

There was ample room for dreams in so many thousands of square miles of silent emptiness, and Mr. Wickersham had his own plans for conquest. A youngster named Dick Sears in Mrs. Wickersham's home town, Minneapolis, had given him the idea. Young Sears had a tidy little business selling watches by mail, and intended some day to branch out and go into competition with a successful operation called Montgomery Ward & Company, by putting out a catalog and selling all kinds of things. Mr. Wickersham privately agreed there was room for one more in the mail-order field, and he was confident he could beat young Sears to it. Of course, it would mean moving from Amyville, maybe down to Tucson, so he could have direct access to the transcontinental railway line, but Amyville hadn't lived up to Mr. Wickersham's expectations anyway. Even a man with a habit of winning couldn't pick a winner every time.

Today, though, he thought he had done very nicely in snatching those two fine mules out from under the nose of Undertaker Atkins. He didn't quite like the looks of their papers, but that was a frequent problem with stock bought from Z. Z. Gitz, and Mr. Wickersham had developed a method of dealing with it. Tomorrow one of his teamsters would leave for the western New Mexico circuit. Mr. Wickersham would send the mules along to his fellow forwarding agent there and let them work the New Mexico routes for a time. Until tomorrow, there was his freight yard at the edge of the settlement. It had not only an array of spacious corrals but also a large, secluded barn. They'd be well out of sight there. But it was a pity that he couldn't drive around town that very day with a pair of cherry-red, blue-blooded, genuine George Washington mules.

Panting in the white dust of the road behind him, a tired, troubled dog followed. Why had his own man not been at that place with his mules? Why was this other man taking them somewhere? But the dog would surely find his man at the end of this road. Meanwhile, he was determined not to lose sight of the mules.

Five

ABOVE THE MOUNTAINS northeast of Amyville, massive white puffs of cumulus clouds began to appear, but they brought no new rain. The afternoon's accumulated heat also mounted, attaining an ovenlike 105 degrees as the day burned toward evening, and the dog was hot and hurting. While zigzagging to take advantage of every possible inch of shade, he had picked up cactus spines in his right front paw from a club of prickly pear hidden in the dust. His first act upon reaching Solomon Wickersham's barn at the edge of Amyville was to limp into its shade and delicately nibble out the offending spines with bared incisors, taking care not to touch them with his lips. Once spined in the mouth, he would be able only to foam helplessly.

He could smell nothing distinctly through the hot wood of the barn, but he had seen the mules led inside. Once his paw seemed free of spines, he was driven back to his feet by the mules' tantalizing nearness. He trotted around the barn, seeking entrance, but the teamster who would leave the next day for New Mexico saw the dog as he neared the open barn door and yelled, "Hey you, dawg! Git away!" To show he meant business, the man hurled a rock well aimed not actually to hit the dog, but to sail dangerously close to the rump.

The dog withdrew. First incomprehensibly deserted by his man, then broomed, now chunked. What had happened to humankind? He waited until the teamster left the barn and went into a warehouse, then he waited some more before trotting the other direction around the barn, to try once more for the open door.

He found, instead, a trio of black pigs lying in a cool wallow on the far side of the barn. Although pigs are among the brightest of animals, with a greater understanding of cause and effect than most four-footed creatures, they tend toward instant hysteria when startled. The smallest pig sounded an alarm call to his lounging comrades, one "Oof!" like a coughing bark. All three pigs lurched to their feet, their veneer of intelligence cracking like the caked mud on their backs, and scattered in panic. The largest pig ran so blindly that it bumped headlong into a gnarled mesquite tree, which slowed down its flight. The other two, more fortunate in their chosen escape route, rushed toward the front of the barn, caught up in the sudden contagion of fear.

The dog watched in confusion, not comprehending what had triggered the outburst, then trotted along behind them. He reached the corner in time to see the two front-running pigs dash erratically across the dusty ground leading away from the barn, noisily widening the gap between themselves and the dog. But the third pig, tree-slowed and alone, knew only that some scarcely imaginable terror was at its heels, and it darted, screaming piercingly, through the open barn door.

It plunged past a string of horses loosely tied along a row of feedboxes, and the horses, instantly stricken with the same nameless terror, thrashed against their bonds. The pig darted mindlessly from side to side, then charged into a box stall housing a black mare and a matching filly. The mare kicked at the pig, ears back, teeth bared, so the pig burst back into the center of the barn, shrieks turning into piggy roars. A nervous gelding in a nearby stall leaped halfway out of the stall, then got lodged on the door, all four hoofs off the ground and kicking. A huge brown ox ailing with an infected eye lunged to his feet and stumbled against the side of the stall, which half collapsed onto his yokemate, housed next door for company's sake. Both oxen stuck out their tongues and bellowed in fright.

34

They battered against their stall doors. The clatter and clamor were enough to finish the job on the skittish horses at the feed-boxes. Three jerked loose and pounded toward daylight, almost colliding with the dog at the door. The dog cringed to one side as the horses bolted past him.

Inside and out, havoc broke loose. Throughout the extensive network of corrals, the barn and sundry sheds, panic became pandemonium and animals exploded in all directions. A terrified rooster with a green tail scuttled down the street, heading toward the center of Amyville, and four horses from a neighboring corral, having broken through a rickety gate, stampeded after him. From inside the barn came even more horses, then the two oxen which had finally succeeded in battering their way to freedom. They came in spurts and herds, some heading for open country across the back of the freight lot, some winging down the dusty road toward L. L. Gitz's isolated hotel, others galloping along the street to Amyville, following the rooster and its entourage.

The dog was as alarmed as his bellowing, squawking fellows. He uttered a *ki-yip* and retreated from the center of chaos with his stubby tail between his legs. He heard a loud shout from the teamster in the warehouse, then a more distant shout at the edge of Amyville, then a chorus of shouting from even deeper in Amyville rising above the spreading confusion. But one sound among all the others caught him up short—the frightened braying of a young mule. He turned to see the younger of his two mules, Young Jeb, emerge from the barn on the heels of Old Jeb. Both mules headed away from town.

The dog rushed after them, more for self-protection than from a desire to protect the mules. Old Jeb recognized the dog, but warned him away with a lashing of the tail that meant a kick would follow if he didn't keep his distance. The dog dropped willingly enough behind, but still he followed. Together, the three of them galloped off toward open country-side.

35

Four blocks away, Dr. Harold J. DeMeyers began coughing from the dust kicked up by succeeding waves of decamping animals. He hurried to his front door to see what the commotion was about and found his resident patient already there, smiling through the open door at a panting teamster who was laughing his head off, apparently not at all perturbed that his employer's stock was running away. A voice in back of the teamster howled, "Watch it! Here comes some more!" Hoofbeats pounded. Another voice shouted, "Catch 'em!" It was Solomon Wickersham. The teamster wheeled and chased down the street with Mr. Wickersham, and Dr. DeMeyers gasped, "Close that door! The dust!"

His patient looked apologetic, and he looked even more so when Dr. DeMeyers lectured him for being out of bed. No matter that the young man claimed to be feeling well. There could still be slow bleeding inside the skull at the impact point. But the teamster, no longer laughing, chose that moment to tear back up the street in front of a huge sow, its mean red eyes glittering and its yellow teeth gnashing at his heels, and Dr. DeMeyers had to stop lecturing and laugh with the patient.

So the patient was still there when Z. Z. Gitz bustled in with his brother L. L. and blurted, "If that wasn't those two George Washington mules we just glimpsed, I'll eat my suspenders. Scampering out of town like Apaches were after them. And us just come in to bring you your split. Sol Wickersham took them off my hands for seventy-five dollars each. I didn't get what I hoped, but—"

"Er," said Dr. DeMeyers. He gestured, he hoped discreetly, at his patient.

Perhaps Z. Z. didn't recognize the nightshirted young man, one arm and hand in a cast, as the unconscious photographer he had encountered with the mules in the canyon, for he reached into his pocket and continued, "The way they were running, there was no hope of catching them, us with just the buckboard, or I'll bet I could have sold them twice. But here's your seventy-five. I should have got more. I even had Wickersham convinced they were genuine George Washington stock, whereas any fool could see they were everyday Texas bays. But that's mule trading for you."

"Uh, I beg your pardon," Dr. DeMeyers' patient said uneasily, "but . . . two Texas bays? I got two Texas bay mules. You couldn't by any chance . . . ?"

It still might have been all right, Dr. DeMeyers thought, had not Solomon Wickersham butted in. He appeared suddenly from the vacant lot, a roped horse in tow. One of his hired hands was disappearing toward the freight yard with a larger catch, three black mules and a big brown ox, and Mr. Wickersham called to the hand to take the horse. Then he popped his head in Dr. DeMeyers' door and said hurriedly, "You haven't seen a black mare with a filly, have you? She bites. Oh, Gitz. Doggone it, man, come help me. Those two bay mules you sold me were last seen heading for the widow Swagerty's melon field. They mess up that biddy's melons and I'm out a bundle."

Z. Z. looked alarmed. "Yes, indeedy," he said. "L. L., you go right along with Mr. Wickersham, and I'll follow behind in a second or two."

"Two bay mules?" Dr. DeMeyers' patient said again.

Mr. Wickersham sagged against the door frame, resting a moment. He nodded. "Some darn dawg got into my pigs, and everything broke loose. And wouldn't you know it'd be getting dark? With Pimas and Papagos all over the place, not to mention those blasted Apaches that're always whooping off from San Carlos, I'll be lucky to round up half my stock."

"You say a dog too, sir?" asked the patient anxiously. "Dr. DeMeyers, you couldn't by any chance . . . ? Well, no, I do beg your pardon. I couldn't have misunderstood you, could I, all cracked on the head and all? My dog and my mules, I guess they *are* being looked after and doing just fine, aren't they?"

Z. Z. snapped to full attention. "Oh, say, did we say Texas

bays? We meant Virginia bays," he said, backpedaling clumsily.

But Dr. DeMeyers knew defeat when he met it. For him, it was a frequent encounter. He shook his head and said, "It's no use, Mr. Gitz. Mr. Wickersham, it looks like we have a little something to straighten out here. Mr. Fairchild, I'm afraid there has been a misunderstanding about your, er, state of finances and your animals. You see . . ."

Z. Z. Gitz could see that Doc DeMeyers' patient was very disturbed. So was Solomon Wickersham, from the way he looked when he left. So was L. L., but who knew whether it was because of that unsullied conscience L. L. was always droning about, or the simple fear of getting clapped in jail? Z. Z. cringed mentally. Amyville's jail was a one-room, dirt-floored affair.

It was all the doc's fault, he decided indignantly, listening to them chatter away. Hadn't the doc led him to believe the photographer fellow was on the verge of going to his reward? Or, if not conveniently dying, at least sure to be sick so long that the transaction would have been long settled before he was in any position to object? Talk about bad luck. Who would ever have dreamed the shabbily dressed young fellow would have been so completely capable of paying his own medical tab?

Of course, the fellow kept saying the only important thing was to find the mules and the dog, but Z. Z. knew what he must really have in mind. He'd sic the law on them sure unless those mules were found. Or demand payment for them. Z. Z. cringed again. No question about it, he'd already have to pay back the full purchase price to Solomon Wickersham. But he couldn't possibly face paying the photographer for them too. Should he confess to DeMeyers he had shaded their price a little? Unthinkable. The alternative might be for DeMeyers to pony up only an additional seventy-five dollars, which he probably didn't even have, and for him, Z. Z., to have to come

38

up with the rest out of his very own pocket. But the mules would be found. They had to be.

As much to console himself as the photographer fellow, Z. Z. interrupted Dr. DeMeyers' interminable excuses and said, "I'll eat my pocket watch if those mules aren't back in Wickersham's barn this very night."

But trust the doc to keep the photographer all stirred up, for the fellow only looked more anxious when DeMeyers said, "Or maybe they're already on their way home. Animals do that, you know. Where do you live, Mr. Fairchild? Prescott? Tucson? Or somewhere closer, I'll bet."

The fellow seemed to sputter or stutter, and then the words came stumbling out. "I've got me a little place near Salida, Colorado," he said worriedly, "but the animals have only been there twice, and I've already been on the road four months since the last time. I expect they don't even remember it. No, sir, the mules are from Denison City, Texas, and that poor old dog, I guess he's from Temple, Texas, or around. But he lived on the road with his master, mainly, and then his master died. Poor old boy, he don't have anywhere to go back to. I sure wish I'd kept them home in Salida. Old Nemo liked it there. No, sir, I just got to rent me a horse and go out and scour the countryside around for them."

"I assure you, Mr. Fairchild, we'll find the animals for you," Dr. DeMeyers said. "You'll risk worsening that head injury if you try to go out."

"I've just got to," the photographer said. "When I think of what the others will say . . . My cousin and my friends, they never wanted old Nemo to go with me, rambling the way I do. But I told them I'd look after him. Now look what I've done. I sure wish you'd told me, Dr. DeMeyers, when the boy you sent couldn't find him."

"I'm awfully sorry," the doc said. "I was afraid it would worry you."

"Yes, sir, it does."

Z. Z. said, with perfect sincerity, "We'll all go to looking for

39

them at first light. The direction those mules were headed when me and my brother drove in, I'll eat my britches if we don't find them back in that canyon. The dawg too. He's probably been there all the time. Probably just wouldn't come to a strange boy. Dawgs are like that. But he'll come a-running and a-wriggling when he hears you, you betcha."

"I don't know that he would," the photographer said sadly. "He always minded me good, but he never did warm up to me all that much. Looked like he never quite got over missing his master."

"Of course he'll be happy to see you," Dr. DeMeyers said reassuringly. With a glance at Z. Z., he attempted levity. "I'll eat my own britches if the mules aren't waiting in Wickersham's corral and the dog in the canyon in the morning. Tonight, we must get you to bed, Mr. Fairchild."

"That's right," said Z. Z. "Nothing a good night's rest can't help."

Z. Z. said his good nights. As he stepped into the street, he heard a sudden flurry of hoofbeats, then the sound of glass breaking down toward the Cosmopolitan Restaurant. Brightening, he turned toward it. Given a little luck, it would be those two blasted would-be George Washington mules pushing some citizen through a store window.

Given a little luck, the mules would have drifted with the second ox and sundry other of Solomon Wickersham's stock into the melon field cultivated by the Irish widow near the settlement, their hoofs and appetites creating seventeen dollars' worth of damages, which Wickersham paid with a groan the next morning. The mere fact that the dog was chasing them, however, kept the young mule on the run. The twilight deepened. Finally Old Jeb slowed and stopped. He paid no attention to Young Jeb's nervous wish to gallop on. He just stopped, because it was the sensible thing to do.

The dog caught up, and Old Jeb turned to face him with ears erect and toothy mouth open, a mule's calm greeting. All

40

three were winded and thirsty. There was no water near, or they would have drunk. Instead, Old Jeb sniffed out a patch of bare ground, then flopped down and rolled. He rolled first on one side, then conscientiously on the other, until his red hide was as whitely powdered as the wig of the distinguished forefather with whom Z. Z. Gitz had provided him. He stood and shook, filling the dog's eyes with clouds of grit, then rolled again. Young Jeb returned and watched him solemnly. When Old Jeb had cleaned and polished his sweat-soaked hide to his satisfaction, the young mule lay down and began a dozen rolls of his own.

For his part, the dog flopped down and panted, cooling his body through the evaporation of moisture from his lungs and throat. This soon made him thirstier. He suffered as the mules began quietly grazing, but he was too tired to go on.

For two hours the animals rested. A quarter-moon crept through the sky, adding to the light of the stars. For animals whose actual forebears were night hunters and night hunted, the light intensity, though low, was adequate.

Had the mules broken from Amyville on the south road toward the Gitz Hot Springs Hotel, the dog might not have had the happy thought of the canyon and the wagon. But his sense of direction, when he had rested enough to consider such things, told him that they were well on the way to both. There was water in the canyon. There had always been food from the wagon. Besides, it was one of his charges, and it wasn't proper for the mules and the wagon to be separated. The old dog rose without further delay and made an abrupt lunge at Old Jeb's heels, startling him a few feet farther toward the canyon.

Young Jeb was still seeing ghosts, and it took dozens of lunges to start them moving steadily in the right direction, but then Old Jeb seemed to consider the wisdom of the dog's course of action and allowed himself to be herded onward. As always, the young mule followed his work mate. They soon intersected the two ruts that served as the eastward road passing the canyon, and after that it was easy going. Old Jeb paused and lashed his tail warningly at the ford where the canyon's streamlet met the ruts. He drank lengthily. So did the dog and Young Jeb, and then the dog moved them on toward the wagon.

It was only a short way. The dog dashed ahead of the mules, suddenly confident that the wagon would now contain his man.

In the almost total darkness under the cottonwoods, his nose told him what his eyes couldn't. There was no man. Now, there was not even the wagon. There was only his iron skillet, forgotten, lying empty on the ground.

Fear can overwhelm a lost animal to the point that it goes into what resembles a state of shock. Fear can cause temporary paralysis. Fear can somehow wash all previously learned lessons from an animal's brain, and a dog running from a burning building may fail to come when called not only because of terror but because it apparently has forgotten everything it knew, even this first and simplest command.

And for the first time, the old dog felt profoundly afraid. His safe, familiar existence under the wheels of the wagon was gone. He was hungry. Even after resting, he was tired. The canyon no longer had any slight feeling of home. The sea of darkness surrounding him suddenly nudged him, tentatively, like a feeding shark.

But then came the footsteps of the mules, unhurried, moving nearer. The fear ebbed. In the next moment the dog experienced a comforting sensation of being in a kitchen, the one with the cold-water stream outside and the warm stove inside to lie beside and twitch and dream.

Where the sensation came from, he had no way of knowing. It was strong, yet vague, shifting and formless as a dream. Was his master lying awake, worrying, perhaps even thinking at that moment of the kitchen? Some humans thought animals could read minds, particularly if you happened to picture something in your thoughts. They were forever telling how old Drum would flee under the house or Lady escape through the

42

door the minute the idea of bathing the dog occurred to them. They even thought mind-reading might be how some tattered cat showed up at her family's new, never-seen home in Oklahoma Territory after being left a thousand weary miles behind in Ohio, or why a dog suddenly put his nose in the air and howled dismally at just the moment his master was killed in a train accident hundreds of miles away.

It can't be said that the old dog really thought about his dilemma, much less tried to make a plan. He merely had the thought of the kitchen, and, tired as he was, he instantly bounded toward the mules and snapped at their heels just enough to start them slowly up the canyon. A mountain lay north, but so did that kitchen, and perhaps he would find it over this very mountain.

He didn't know or care that he was lost and that nearly five hundred miles of the wildest country in the whole Southwest lay between him and the one place that could give him refuge —a mountain cabin seen only twice. Despite what his newest master thought, it was the place to which he had already decided he must drive the mules. He never doubted that there they would all be together again. Then he would be home.

Six

LIKE AN ISLAND, the first range of mountains rose greenly from the brown desert floor. The dog and the two mules climbed to an autumnlike freshness, for season and climate in the desert changed predictably with each hundred feet or so of altitude. By daybreak, the spiny growth of cactus and palo verde had given way to chaparral. By the time the sun grew hot and the dog felt his strength giving out, they were in Ponderosa pine and fir.

The mules seemed glad to rest. Their preference was to sleep during the hottest part of a day, then feed, drink, and conduct their social affairs during the cooler hours and the night. Reasonable work, when it was imposed on them, was accepted with resignation or, on the part of at least Old Jeb, with a critical interest. Knowing the ways of mules, the farmer with his mule and forty acres usually allotted a compromise rest period from eleven in the morning until two in the afternoon, but the dog had much to learn. He slept an hour, then, eager to get on home, stiffly regained his feet. The trees here seemed sparse and dry. They were thick and lush near his kitchen. The air was wrong, the sounds were wrong, the position of the sun was wrong. Obviously he would have to herd the mules a little farther along.

Old Jeb refused to move. The dog herded with his head low, chin almost resting on the ground so that any kicks would go over his head, and it was just as well, for Old Jeb lashed out at him, then stood nodding his head rhythmically, warning

45

the dog to desist. Old Jeb was busy eating. He chose a mouth-ful or two of grass. Then he moved a few steps toward a bog into which a spring seeped, there to eat a bitter, white-petaled marsh marigold with a golden center. Then he stepped deeper into the bog to a hollow and drank a few swallows of water. Then it was back to the grass to start all over again, slowly, deliberately, a serious business with which he wanted no inter-ference.

The dog paused and watched carefully. His basic problem with the mules was simply that they didn't speak the same language. Both species used body language as their primary means of communicating, but there were major differences. The dog had learned some things. A waving tail didn't mean the same thing to a dog and a mule, although it might to a mule and an irritated cat. For the most part, though, he was stuck with the kind of vocabulary in which a traveler could laboriously piece out, "Where is the cathedral, please?" but never be able to understand the answer.

Too, moderation was a virtue to a mule, whether it was in plowing or in traveling. Old Jeb made it very apparent that he not only intended to dine but to enjoy a good long snooze. Young Jeb awoke to eat and serve as lookout and Old Jeb went to sleep, standing, and the dog soon gave up his attempts to budge them. He was hungry too, and he went to see what he could do about it.

Summer rains had come to these dry mountains as well as to the flats below. Harebells stood tall among the grass, bright blue flowers nodding on many of the stalks. Nose down and tail stub high, the dog began to cast about among them, hop-ing for fresh scent of game.

After thirty minutes he flushed a half-grown jackrabbit, then lost it. In time he flushed one of the jack's litter mates, but he lost it too. Age took its tolls. Unperturbed, the dog trailed after lesser game, the tiny, white-footed mouse, and eight mice eventually slid down his gullet. They would keep

46

him going until he got home. He returned to have another go at the mules.

Awake and grazing together, they had drifted upwind, as their kind tended to do when in strange surroundings. The wind was from the south, the direction from which they had come, and the dog realized that he was losing ground. He turned them, but once back near the bog Old Jeb decided to eat again. With a feeling of mounting frustration, the dog waded into the bog and lay down to wait again. Frustration turned to irritation, and the dog was on the verge of nipping the unco-operative mules in earnest when the weather intervened in his favor.

The wind shifted and started to gust. It was enough. Long before the first peal of thunder, both dog and mules knew that a storm was gathering. They could feel it in every hair of their coats, a building charge of electricity in the air. Soon the dog could smell ozone, and after a while even the dull-nosed mules picked it up. They no longer parried the dog's efforts to move them north. Old Jeb still wouldn't hurry. The clouds boiling up to form a ghost mountain were far behind them, and in desert country, rain could fall by the buckets in one locale while thirsty ground a quarter mile away wouldn't get a drop. But Old Jeb plodded north at a steady pace, leading the way for Young Jeb, who followed nose to tail, and leaving the dog little to do but bring up the rear. They left the storm behind. The dog got tired long before the mules did. By nightfall, when the wind shifted and Old Jeb started to drift upwind again, the dog was flagging badly. But down this next draw, across this next stream, he was still certain he would meet a skilletful of softened jerked beef and a mountain cabin with a wagon parked alongside.

At nightfall, Calvin Fairchild was forced to call a temporary halt to his search for his missing animals. He left the canyon by starlight, heading back to Amyville. His arm ached, and his head ached, and this was his third circle out to the canyon on a rented mare named Guapa. Although he'd told himself to give up on the canyon, it seemed as though he just couldn't stay away from it. He felt foolish, like a man who keeps looking through his desk for a letter that had slipped out of his pocket at the post office, and he felt very, very worried. He'd turned up no trace at all of Nemo and the Jebs. That lady at the Hot Springs Hotel, yes, she'd seen the Jebs, since that rascally brother-in-law of hers had tried to sell them there, but, useless hope, she'd seen no dog, just as her husband had said. The man whose stock had run away, Mr. Wickersham, hadn't either. He'd only heard about a marauding dog from the laughing teamster, who had already left for New Mexico. Like Mr. Wickersham said, there were loose dogs all over Amyville. And, for certain, old Nemo had never been a marauder.

Calvin had been so sure when he set out that morning that he'd find all three animals in the canyon that he'd filled his pockets with jerked beef and tied a bag of oats to the back of the saddle. At the ford, higher now from rain in the mountains, he suddenly pulled up on Guapa's reins. The tired mare mouthed the bit and danced sideways, anxious for stall and feedbag. Calvin dithered. Shouldn't he at least go back to where the wagon had been and leave the food on the ground? Maybe they'd wander back there at night.

Guapa jerked her head and tried to wade into the ford, and Calvin sighed and let her go. Fool thought. Nemo had probably left the canyon two days back when Calvin had first hurt himself scrambling to take an unnecessary view. The poor old dog. Wandering somewhere, starving by now. Could he possibly have gone south, heading all the way back for Texas? Calvin could scarcely bear to think about it. But tomorrow, when he could begin to search again, he would watch and call and ask south.

The northbound order of march for the dog and mules was quickly established. When the wind was from the north, the mules wandered upwind readily and the dog had only to follow, but if the wind switched, as it tended to do quickly in broken country, it was back to work and snapping at their heels. He was afraid to rest much. The mules' intervals of deep sleep were brief and irregular, and the rest of the time they were apt to awaken to feed and meander off in the wrong direction again. He was afraid as well to take out much time for hunting, but that was no great problem until they descended the north face of the first mountain range, for grass was plentiful and therefore so were the mice and ground squirrels which thrived on grass seed. There was nothing wrong, either, with a few fat grasshoppers, which could often be caught as he trotted along.

True hunger began on the downward trek, back to the floor of the desert. The route was no problem. The dog followed game trails, and the game trails followed alongside water, and the water carved natural passes through the rocky folds of the mountains. The old problem of the wind did arise, though. In the long canyon the dog chose for their exit, it blew upcanyon in the morning but downcanyon in the evening, and the mules veered as senselessly as weather vanes, causing more loss of time. It was not that the mules lacked the homing urge so often seen in birds and other animals. It was only that their recognition of home territory depended heavily on wind-borne clues, and failing any familiar scents, they walked upwind anyway. The demands of herding left the dog no leisure for hunting. And once to the mouth of the exit canyon he was back in spine-and-sticker country and game was no longer as plentiful.

By the end of the first week, they were climbing again, although gradually. The ground rose inexorably, and the desert fauna began subtly to change. No more giant saguaros appeared. Low desert was giving way to high. They came to a formidable canyon, in which ran a red, muddy river matching steep red walls that broke to disclose a jumble of mesas and side canyons, then another canyon, then another, brown and rust and red, fading off hazily to mauve, to lavender, to shadowed blue, under a vast and empty sky. All that day and the next they traveled up through the canyon. Cedar trees became common. Old Jeb discovered that the dog was heading in a specific direction, northeast. In his workmanlike way, the mule curtailed his windward meanderings and began to co-operate, which made traveling easier. The dog forgot each day as it passed, and his expectations remained high of soon encountering his own lush aspens and the correct position of sun and stars.

They were out of the big canyon and into a mere side canyon when the next rainstorm came. At dawn, the sky was a clear, blue bowl, but soon a faint skim of clouds appeared and then a whole flock of puffy, white, flatbottomed clouds gathered on the eastern horizon. By midday, they dotted the sky from horizon to horizon and were thickening. A mile-long cloud passed between the animals and the sun, the first of many, and the transient shade kept Old Jeb plodding later into the day than usual. Then he looked for deeper shade and a good place to sleep, finding it in a wide arroyo floored gaudily with red sand. There was no water, but the mules could withstand heat and thirst better than horses, or, for that matter, dogs. Old Jeb ate a little dry grass, then bent his knees and hocks with the slow majesty of a king kneeling, and he lay down in the shade of the bank. Scrubby cedars grew atop the bank. Young Jeb moved into their shade and dozed on his feet. As usual, he was sentry for the first shift.

The dog licked his abraded paws for a long while, then he slept too. Overhead, the thick clouds hazed together, losing discreteness, and to the north, up the big canyon, innocent-looking cumulus clouds began to mass, setting the stage for a curious phenomenon.

The phenomenon had begun four days before in the Gulf of Mexico, when a hurricane swept toward the Mexican mainland a little north of Tampico. Thirty-two people drowned be-

50

fore the storm broke up, and a great new stream of moist tropical air met and melded in the upper atmosphere with a warm, wet air river already sweeping in from the Caribbean. The merged air stream was twenty thousand feet deep. Thus the stage was set. A few isolated thunderstorms took place as the great air river entered southern Arizona, and the air lost much of its load to an offshoot that swept off to bludgeon the Bradshaw Mountains, but much moisture remained to rise on vertical currents within towering clouds. The higher a droplet rose, the colder it became, until finally it froze. Other droplets were attracted to the tiny mass. It got so big that the violent air current could no longer keep it up, and down it fell, colliding with other droplets, gathering them in, and eventually melted. To the scorched ground, a raindrop fell.

Far up the canyon, a slate-colored junco in a cedar tree stirred nervously long before a low grumble of thunder rolled. The sky darkened, and the light turned a dull yellow, and the junco moved to a lower branch. A ground squirrel scuttled for its burrow. Forked lightning ripped the sky, followed by more thunder. A heavy silence fell.

Suddenly, a red dust devil forty feet high whirled by, then came the real wind and its burden of red, wind-blown sand. The junco's cedar tree groaned and bent as the bird cowered, eyes closed against the stinging sand, on the tree's sheltered side. Then the great rainstorm hurled itself against the land, annihilating even the wind.

The column of rain, visible for thirty or forty miles, as such desert storms often are, soon passed on. So did the deluge of rainwater, running downhill in drops that became trickles, then rivulets, finally a red, roaring wave crashing down the canyon at terrifying speed. At the head of the long arroyo in which the dog and two mules slept, it slammed against a wall of vermilion sandstone, and a lesser wave, only four or five feet high, diverted itself into the arroyo. On it tumbled, devouring boulders, bushes, and sand that a moment before had been dry, bearing on its crest the corpse of an occasional tree.

51

Entangled in the branches of one, a slate-colored junco, dead, bobbed and plunged.

Young Jeb, napping lightly, reacted like a good sentry to the first distant roar of the wave. He snorted, the mule's danger signal to the herd, and Old Jeb and the dog both were immediately up, then running. Old Jeb seemed to realize he could never hope to outgallop the wave. After only a few feet he plunged up the bank, Young Jeb right behind him. The dog tried to follow. He might have made it, but a cedar branch, slapping back after Young Jeb crashed through it, caught him in the eyes, and the water rushed below him.

It instantly ate out the soft dirt of the bank up which he was attempting to scramble. The ground collapsed beneath the dog's thrashing paws, and the water rolled over him.

Caught by the first wave, he would have been quickly crushed by the churning rocks and debris it carried. But the moment that it took the powerful grinder to chew the bank carried the crest of the flood eighty feet down the arroyo, and the great danger the dog faced was drowning. He swam stoutly for a heartbeat of time, then a swell raised him higher and trembled beneath him and broke, all in the next heartbeat. The dog was hurled downward, tumbled, somersaulted deep into the grinding turbulence.

The dog's back scraped bottom, his paws thrashing above his head. He twisted back to the surface just in time for another swell to dash him down again, smashing him helplessly beneath its vast weight. It rolled him until he didn't know up from down. He gulped water. Then he felt air. It came and went so quickly that he failed to gulp then, and he was down again, then up, rearing and bucking on the turbulent surface of the water.

The junco's cedar tree got him to the edge of the flood. It slammed into his side and swept him against a steep, muddy bank, then swept onward, while the dog paddled desperately to stay where he was. He tried to cling to the bank, but a dog's paw is ill suited for grasping. The pads and claws slipped again and again. Thrashing, swimming almost upright, he was quickly becoming exhausted.

Downstream, the taproot of yet another cedar tree beckoned. This was not the first flash flood to race down the arroyo, and the cedar, roots once snugly sunk into earth, now stood on the edge of an eroding bank a few yards from the dog. In the next flood it might topple. Its long, snaky taproot was already exposed, stretching down to disappear into the sanded floor of the arroyo. This was not even the worst gully-washer, for the cedar and the top of the bank were several feet above the water line, too high for the dog to lunge and too steep for him to climb. But the tangle of roots was there.

Weakening, the old dog thrashed even more wildly. All claws slipped at once, leaving him at the mercy of the current. By simple accident, the dog was washed into the roots. Once there he clung.

When he could, he struggled up the slippery network of roots. The water rolled more quietly beneath him. Perhaps by now he could have paddled to an easier place to get out, but he was terrified of the water. He climbed and slipped and rested and climbed some more. One forepaw, then the other, finally scrabbled over the top of the bank. It was dry. No single raindrop had fallen here. He dragged himself up, then as far away as he could from the red, calmly rolling water. There was a rock. He crawled up against it and collapsed. His eyes closed. His breath came in erratic shudders.

It would be a long, long time before he would be able to remember the mules.

Seven

THE YOUNG OWNER of the missing dog and mules could tell that even Mr. Solomon Wickersham, who had been most wonderfully helpful to him, regarded him as a little touched in the head. And as for the gaunt, melancholy Dr. DeMeyers, a worried frown seemed to cross his face every time he looked at Calvin. Yet it seemed so obvious to Calvin that he must cut short his current view-taking tour and go directly to Texas. Even if the hope was remote that one or all of the animals might turn up there, he had to pursue it.

They'd all tried to calculate how fast and how far the animals might travel. Two and a half miles an hour for mules pulling a wagon and easily twice that trotting free if they cared to move at all smartly, said Mr. Wickersham. As for distance and direction, without a human urging them on, there was no telling. It was his experience that once an animal got five or ten miles from home, it couldn't seem to find its way back again. Mr. Wickersham wasn't sure even dogs could make out direction and reason their way to it until Calvin told him about Mr. Harmon A. Berry's Gyp back home in Louisiana who once ran a fox from Dorcheat Bayou across the line and clean up to Black Springs, Arkansas. He was seen there by a man who recognized him and tried to catch him, but the dog shied away and three days later was back home, and that was a distance of a hundred forty-four and seven-tenths miles, either going or coming.

Still, there was no telling whether Calvin's animals had set out with any particular destination in mind, whether they'd go straight to Denison City, or straight to Temple, or straight anywhere. The only sure thing was, they weren't around Amyville—if, after all the searching, he could be absolutely sure even of that. Nor could Calvin rule out the possibility that old Nemo might have remembered Tombstone, where Calvin and the dog had first come to belong to each other. Calvin—and the dog—had good friends who still lived there. Tombstone was nearest, and Mr. Wickersham had a freight shipment going south, with plenty of room, Mr. Wickersham claimed, on the wagons. So that was where Calvin was going first. Then he'd catch the Southern Pacific in Tucson and try the enormous expanse of Texas. "A needle in a haystack," Dr. DeMeyers had said last night, shaking his head. But Mr. Z. Z. Gitz had said, "My own mother once found a gold collar button my own father lost in a haystack, and if I'm not telling you the truth I'll eat my socks." Mr. Z. Z. Gitz had been downright accommodating, especially after Calvin had refused payment for his lost mules.

In fact, Mr. Z. Z. Gitz was paying for having Calvin's traveling photographic studio hauled to his mountain cabin in Colorado, since Calvin didn't know how long it would be before he would be making portraits and views again. Calvin wanted to pay for that, but Mr. Wickersham said no, Mr. Gitz had already insisted. So the big blue wagon stood that morning in Mr. Wickersham's freight yard, waiting for a northbound shipment, and a letter had gone off to Calvin's best friend in Salida, Postmaster Robert Elford, a fellow harelip. The letter asked him to please receive the wagon and have it parked by the cabin, and it told Calvin's change of itinerary because he was going off in search of old Nemo and the Jebs. Calvin hated to put his friend out that way, and he hoped someday he could find some way of returning the favor.

Calvin hoped the same about the new friends who had gone to so much trouble for him. His was a forgiving nature, and it

56

worried him that Dr. DeMeyers and Mr. Z. Z. Gitz kept looking so uncomfortable. They'd both come to see him off. Dr.
DeMeyers leaned coughing against one of Mr. Wickersham's
tandem wagon rigs, and Mr. Gitz sat on the top rail of a corral
and watched Mr. Wickersham helping the teamster, an older
man with the kind of vocabulary that preachers wrote heated
sermons about, as the teamster checked the harness straps on
the twelve-mule team. The veteran lead mules calmly stood
swishing flies, their liquid, intelligent eyes looking full of self-
importance. Although black, they reminded Calvin of Old
Jeb, and he let a sigh escape him.

Dr. DeMeyers came over to him immediately. "Mr. Fairchild, I still have severe misgivings about all this activity
you're contemplating," he said. "Are you sure your head isn't
still bothering you?"

"Oh, no," Calvin lied. The headaches, though bad, only
came occasionally, and they seemed to be wearing off. Calvin
was more worried about the fact that he sometimes felt dazed
for a moment or two and his memory developed queer gaps at
such times. Just the previous night he had gone to the livery
stable to settle up for Guapa's rent and had suddenly found
himself out in the street, with no recollection of actually paying Mr. Woodruff until he checked his pockets and found he
had subtracted the correct sum. Calvin was afraid to ask Dr.
DeMeyers about it, because he knew he'd just get another lec-
ture about plentiful rest and lengthy quiet. Besides, like the
headaches, it would wear off.

Dr. DeMeyers looked dissatisfied, but he only said, "About
the cast on your arm, don't let some quack get hold of it. I've
seen perfectly knit fractures broken all over again by pressure
improperly applied when removing the cast. Go to a good doctor. The cast should come off in twelve more days."

"Yes, sir," Calvin said, "I'll sure remember that."

"There's another little thing," Dr. DeMeyers said. He
looked down. His hand held out a slip of paper. "This is the
name of the most skillful surgeon in Philadelphia. You may

57

remember I mentioned the operation a good man could do on your lip. I've taken the liberty of writing him about you. If you could ever find the time . . . I mean, it's rather a distance, but if you could . . ."

Calvin's first thought was of his friend Rob Elford in Salida. Wouldn't he be glad to know there was a fine doctor who might be able to fix his lip too? He beamed at Dr. DeMeyers. "Now that's about the nicest thing I ever heard of," he said. "I don't know when I'd ever have a chance to go to Philadelphia, but I just can't tell you how much I appreciate you thinking of it."

"It's nothing man," Dr. MeMeyers said. "But you must try to make the chance to go."

Then it was soon time to say good-by. Calvin climbed into a wagon filled with Santa Claus Soap and assorted clocks. Mr. Wickersham warned the teamster one more time about jostling either the clocks or Calvin. The teamster climbed onto the off-wheel mule, took the jerk line in his one hand and poised his long whip in the other. He gave a sour look over his shoulder to Calvin, and Calvin smiled and said, "Now don't you worry about me. I'm used to jostling."

"Huh?" said the teamster. Calvin tried to repeat it, but the teamster shrugged impatiently and asked Mr. Wickersham, in language as vile as that he would shortly be using on the mules, what the this-and-that the fellow in the wagon was talking about.

Calvin's smile was a little tremulous as he waved his farewells to Amyville. Looked like at least half the world couldn't understand him when he opened his fool mouth to talk. Maybe someday he should find the time to go to Philadelphia and the fine doctor after all. But that would have to wait until he'd found poor old Nemo and the Jebs.

In the arroyo near which the dog lay, most of the floodwater ran off quickly. Only in occasional bends of the bed did puddles remain. They began slowly to dry, and the dog's waterlogged coat also gave up its moisture to the thirsty air. Long, slow tremors passed rhythmically through his body. His eyes remained closed until well into the night, and his teeth were locked in a frozen grin. In his terror, his anal glands had emptied themselves, and an acrid, pungent smell lingered about him. The dog was unaware of it. He was aware of nothing tangible at all. His mind, so like a human's in its inner workings, had retreated from the terror and shock, leaving his body limp and immobile. In the first great world war, soldiers would call it shell shock. In the animal world, where it was common, the paralyzed state may have been a primitive form of "playing possum," going so limp when attacked that any marauder might consider the prey as dead and leave it alone, as predators sometimes did. When the desert night grew cool, the old dog still lay against the rock to which he had dragged himself.

If the night brought no comfort to the dog, it brought joy to other creatures. A hideous, honking sound suddenly rent the air, and once started it went on and on. Soon more nasal honks joined it. From nowhere, from the earth in which they had buried themselves after a torrential thunderstorm the previous summer, dozens of small toads had suddenly appeared, hurrying for the puddles. They had little time. Before the puddles dried, the toads had to lead an entire life span—summon one another, conduct their amorous affairs, deposit fertilized eggs and depart, leaving the eggs to hatch some twenty-four hours later into tadpoles, which had to make haste to turn into toadlets and dig themselves into the mud, all before the last drops of water were gone.

This season the toads were fortunate. Their honkings and *phaah-phaah-phaah*-ings went on for two nights, as the dog scarcely moved from his rock. He was weak. His hunger was so old that he had almost forgotten it. As the hours passed and his eyes fluttered open to a fixed stare, he began to suffer from thirst, but he was too weak to seek water and still too terrified of the arroyo even to consider seeking it in the only place it existed. It was near daybreak on the third day when the thirst helped bring him out of his torpid state. He staggered to his feet and shook himself and whined for a long time, smelling the water, before he finally moved along the bank, then made a plunge downward to a foot-wide, shallow puddle.

Drinking helped. The dog ingested a jellied mass of toad eggs as he drank, hardly noticing them, and they did no harm. He tottered to the next puddle, then was moving on more strongly to the next when a few slate-colored feathers caught his attention. He nosed them hopefully, but the few ounces of the junco's flesh had long since been consumed by other predators. Hunger returned overwhelmingly, and with it apprehension. The dog scrambled back out of the arroyo, feeling more like himself again, and without looking back he began to cast about for any scent of game. And then finally it occurred to him that he was all alone.

He pricked his ears, and beneath his shag his forehead creased into a worried expression. He had not been alone before. He couldn't really remember the wave of red water and wouldn't have wished to if he could, but he did remember clearly that he hadn't been alone. Water and time had removed all faint scent of the mules, or the memory of them might have come rushing back, but now the dog couldn't even remember who had been his comrades. He stopped and stared to the north and whimpered low in his throat. Something faint . . . something . . . Whatever it was, it was quickly gone, and only the empty sky remained. He cowered beneath it.

In the dog's weakened state, panic could have completed what the flood had begun. Lost, weak, and utterly disoriented, he had only one strong urge—his fully awakened hunger—left to drive him on. That it drove him north was not fully an accident. The faint call had come from that direction. Panting as the sun grew stronger, the dog put his nose to the ground and his bobtail as high in the air as he could get it and wandered

60

north, thinking mice, thinking rabbits, thinking carrion, thinking anything to fill the numb void that was his stomach.

Atop the high tableland, the country grew dryer and even emptier. The only green was the grass in the dry washes and the rank growth of tumbleweeds, and at first the dog's only companion was a solitary crow which followed him for two days, perhaps solely out of curiosity, then finally flapped away toward a distant clutter of mesa and butte. The dog then came upon two steel rails stretching endlessly toward the northeast, his own direction, and within the space of five miles he found two crushed rabbits on the tracks.

He traveled on beside the tracks, even after a screaming locomotive roared past him, on its way from Chicago to California. That night, the great glaring eye and roar of another train charged out of the darkness and away. In the morning, the tracks offered up fresh carrion.

When the mesmerizing light of the train failed the dog, his mileposts were his infrequent meals. He ate three chipmunks that had been slaughtered by a bobcat, a gourmet which ate only their brains and left the bodies to rot. He ate a female longspur killed by the clownish cannibal of the deserts, a roadrunner, which the dog managed to frighten away. He caught a gopher on his own, but a badger easily frightened him away from it. In the early mornings, he sought the parallel rows of sunflowers that grew along the tracks and hunted sluggish grasshoppers, sun-warming themselves before they were capable of long flight, but the dog was so sluggish himself that he wasted almost as much energy catching them as their tiny bodies gave him. When he finally stumbled across an endless feast stretched in front of him, he was so feeble that he could scarcely take advantage of it. And the feast had a lively desire not to be eaten.

This was a prairie-dog town lying a quarter mile from the railroad tracks. The dog was led to it late one afternoon by a bad-tempered badger which was already being trailed hopefully by a tiny desert fox and, from the air, a hawk. The dog trailed all three. The badger was a renowned hunter, and there was always a chance his fleeing prey would run into someone else's maw. When they reached the prairie-dog encampment, the dog lay licking his sore feet and watching as the badger, blandly unworried either about his hangers-on or the instant disappearance of his prey into their underground city, dug out a nice dinner with his impressive claws. The badger was a tidy eater and left no remains. He waddled away, the fox after him, and the little rodents' heads popped out of a thousand holes, and the dog made his own try.

The dog knew better than to rush. The mounds at the burrow entrances served as lookout posts, and the prairie dogs' watchword was ceaseless vigilance. He slunk as near as he could without setting off the barking cries that gave the succulent little animals their name, then waited for them to resume their normal activities.

They appeared to spend most of their time visiting, popping out of one burrow to the next, while their unwilling hosts yapped to warn them away. Of course, they also ate. For a prairie-dog town, this was a small colony, covering only about ten acres. Even the dwellers of the innermost burrows didn't have to forage too far for food. But although they extended their burrows ever outward, they had to leave their underground safety sometime. The dog had only to wait downwind until one of the creatures was far enough from a hole so he could snap it up before it reached safety.

Or so he thought. He crouched, frozen, watching, inhaling greedily. Not one but three of the heavy-bodied prairie dogs appeared suddenly on an unnoticed mound not fifteen feet from him. They tested the air and crept out another inch or so, short tails rapidly wagging, then after what seemed a lengthy wait they moved again, separating, moving alertly into dry grass. It wiggled, betraying their paths. One prairie dog was now only nine or ten feet from him.

The dog could stand it no longer. He exploded into forward

motion, then pounced, snorting loudly, teeth bared and snapping. They snapped on empty air. The prairie dog vanished into yet another unnoticed hole almost under his plunging paws. While the dog still snorted and snapped, the prairie dog was fleeing deep into its labyrinthian home, guided through the twisting darkness by its sensitive whiskers in the less familiar outer tunnels and by automatic muscle reaction as it reached its better-known haunts. It didn't know it had escaped death. It knew fear of a pursuer, but like all animals it knew little and anticipated nothing of the thing called dying.

Once convinced that he had really lost his prey, the dog reconnoitered the entire area thoroughly, searching out all the openings, but although he waited again, and rushed again, there always seemed to be one more hole. But the four-footed food was here. He continued to wait.

The dog was so intent that the foraging pack of wild dogs was almost upon him before he suddenly caught sight of them and rose with every hair on his back at attention. A mature female was in the lead, and she bounded forward without a moment's pause. She shot past the old dog, almost brushing him, and in that instant each registered the sex of the other. The old dog then ignored her and concentrated on the rest of the pack.

They were plain domestic dogs, come from who knows where and come together who knows how. Wagon trains crossing since the 1850s may have lost or abandoned some of their progenitors. Excess puppies may have been carried off from quick-growing, quick-dying mining camps and left in the wilds to live or die. Indians had had dogs since their own progenitors had crossed the Bering Straits some twelve to fifteen thousand years before, a dog trotting along at their sides. If it must, the domesticated dog can become feral and manage well enough in the wilds in small packs, and this pack appeared to have done just that.

They were a peculiar crew. A certain family resemblance showed in stiff, tan coats, and a certain set of the ears said maybe somewhere back in the bloodline there was a coydog, a cross between dog and coyote. The coats were scruffy and the bodies slender and quick, so the coydog might not have been too far back. But mostly they were peculiar because the pack comprised three full-grown females, a half-dozen pups that might have been four or five months old, and only one male, perhaps a year old.

The old dog turned stiffly to confront the only male, staring intensely toward him. The younger dog looked away, politely, and allowed himself to be approached. He didn't want to be sniffed. He tucked his tail tightly between his legs and wheeled, and the old dog bumped him with his chest. The other two females trotted in. Their tails were wagging, but the old dog, suddenly outnumbered, lowered his bobtail and did some wheeling himself before the ceremonial sniffing of the hindquarters was mutually accomplished.

Then it was the puppies' turn. The situation was very difficult for a dignified, elderly male to contend with, for each big pup had to be sniffed. A stranger, he was an object of fear to them, yet of burning curiosity, and when they finally permitted him to approach them, each rolled over on its back, cringing and squirming, then each instantly leaped up and darted back and forth, torn between timidity and the desire to fawn on him. It was all but impossible to process even the first puppy, while anyone could see that he still had the rest of the pups to attend to. To complicate the ritual of introduction, the lead bitch rushed in and nipped him, and the old dog was forced to wheel and wheel again amid a tangle of importunate noses and paws, while still attempting by a stiff and dignified posture to indicate that he was master of the entire situation.

On the pack's home grounds, the young male dog and even all three bitches might have attacked the old dog viciously, but they were obviously following the food-providing railroad tracks like the old dog, in transit. Some natural disaster? Some rancher aiming down the barrel of a rifle at the older males that normally should have been with the little pack? The discovery of the old dog and the prairie-dog town seemed to

64

negate any plans of traveling on, and the dominant female quickly indicated her desire to hunt by simply leaving her litter, if the puppies were hers, to the mercy of the old dog and trotting off to learn the location of all thousand prairie-dog holes. The old dog extricated himself from the puppies and trotted after her.

Two noses, four ears and eyes and eight feet. How much more efficient they were than only one set of each. One of the females stayed near the puppies and seemed to feel herself the official lookout, and the young male threw himself upon the nearest burrow and began futilely to dig, but the third female added support to the team the old dog and the dominant female formed. Perhaps the work of the digger was not so futile after all, for alarm seemed to travel through all the tunnels. The old dog heard a quick yap from a teammate and looked in time to see a plump prairie dog out in the open and only a plunge away.

He leaped. His mouth closed on warm fur. He shook the little rodent, lightning jerks, breaking its neck, and he ate it in such haste that he half choked. It was blissful to choke as real food lumped its way into his shriveled belly.

A moment before, a living creature. A moment after, warm, life-giving meat. The dog turned an apprehensive look and a warning growl on his teammates while he ate, but he felt no more guilt toward the prairie dog than a human might feel toward a slice of roast beef, hot from the oven and covered with gravy. And neither did his hungry teammates seem to regard his catch with any rancor. There was another quick yap and another fat prairie dog running toward the second female, and like a bullet she was upon her dinner and eating it, salad course first, starting with the vegetable food in its paunch. The old dog grasped their strategy. It was catch as catch can, but you alerted your teammate when game was sighted. The young male, face powdered with dirt, soon came to join them, as did the other female and the pups, and they all hunted to repletion. It was the first of three days' good hunting at the prairie-dog town.

They left only because a man on horseback appeared one noon as they all napped. The man was three or four miles away and the wind said he soon disappeared into the distance, but the one scent of him seemed to make the older female restless. She consistently ignored the noisy, twice-daily trains and their cars of passengers, but a lone man seemed to be different. Later, when the second female would have gone to hunt, the older female growled warningly and she subsided. Still later the young male slipped to the prominence of one of the prairie-dog mounds and began to sniff the air. That was permitted. No signal passed, no conference took place, but shortly thereafter the adult members of the little pack all rose and began to move. The puppies followed. Dogs are social animals, and the old dog unhesitatingly went with the pack.

They traveled well into the night, moving at an easy jog alongside the train tracks. They sent out no scouts, but stayed more or less grouped together. There were frequent detours to investigate markers left by other animals in the form of dried urine or droppings, and where the scent was that of other canids both the old dog and the wild young male carefully lifted a leg and left their own markers atop them. No hunting was allowed. The pups were of an age to chase after anything that stirred, but a growl from the nearest adult always called them back. The older female had considerable regard for the comfort of her feet, and she appeared always to seek the sandiest, least rocky soil as her course. The moment she encountered a wide, nearly dry riverbed that lazed along beside the train tracks, she accepted it as her roadway and from that point on stayed with it.

For the most part, the banks of the riverbed were low, and the bed itself anywhere from fifty to two hundred feet wide, but at an occasional bend the banks steepened. At the first rise of the banks, fear touched the old dog's mind and he looked

66

about nervously. He almost remembered the source of the fear, but the moment passed. He stayed with the pack in the riverbed, which curved and looped and added at least another quarter mile to each two miles of travel, but when you're going no place in particular it doesn't matter when you get there.

And how soothing the sand was. In places it was still damp from the river's brief summer flow, and they encountered water often enough when rock underlay the sand. At one pool a rattler, stalking prey, coiled slowly and darted its long forked tongue at the suddenly alert pack. The nearsighted snake's sensitive olfactory cells were located in its tongue, and it may have found the smell of the dogs repellent, for it coiled more tightly and the quiet of the night suddenly vibrated with the dry, light, yet urgent sound that they all knew said, "Keep away."

They did not drink at that pool. But at the next, the lead female seemed to feel a stop was indicated. She dug a bed next to the bank in dry sand, scraping it here and there with her forepaws, and settled in. The puppies were tired, and they were also getting hungry. The adults ignored their fitful whines. They had eaten well for three days. In their world, food could not be expected merely because the stomach growled hungrily.

In the day that soon came, the pack loitered in the riverbed. The second female killed a rabbit, but she ate it all herself, and the puppies whined futilely and licked her mouth and smelled it over and over again, small noses wrinkling delicately, rediscovering each second what she had been eating. Finally they flopped back into the sand. The old dog, hungry himself, slouched over to smell the female's mouth too.

She stood quietly and let him sniff. Then she cocked tan ears tipped with black and tentatively wagged tan tail, black-edged on its scroungy feathers. She bowed, and thereby invited him to romp. The old dog responded by wagging his own bob-tail and dancing forward, forgetting his years. Although Black Ears was not in a heat cycle, he nevertheless found her quite

67

enchanting, which fact he indicated by bumping her with his neck. The puppies instantly were on their feet and joining in. Playtime! Surely they too were invited. A sharp-toothed pup wound around old Nemo's feet. Five more tumbled after him. The old dog changed his mind and started to flee, but he couldn't very well just surrender with Black Ears standing by, and he paused just long enough for the puppies to swarm all over him. They bit his ears. They bit his lip. They bit his legs. They bit harder than any adult, unless blood was the object, and the dog danced as desperately as his old bones would allow him, trying to defend all four legs at once. In the end he had no option. He scrambled out of the riverbed and fled through greasewood and saltbush growing at the top, leaving victory and sundry tufts of black-and-white hair to the pups.

Black Ears ran after him. The old dog was not gratified by her loyalty. He felt embarrassed, and he preferred no witnesses. Was that a burr he suddenly noticed in a front paw? Yes, surely. He stopped and chewed energetically. Black Ears approached him, but he wouldn't look at her. He disposed of his imaginary burr and cleaned the toes thoroughly, and only then was he ready to pretend that nothing at all had happened, except, oh yes, he had come out here to hunt, so of course he had to sniff every widely spaced saltbush, and check all along the railroad tracks, and if Black Ears wanted to follow, well, no one really cared as long as she didn't interfere with his hunting.

Scent of coyote. Stale scent of small brown rabbit, perhaps the one Black Ears had recently killed. Peculiar reek of black snake, unpleasant to the dog. He moved on to scent of ferret, promising, since ferrets and rattlers and burrowing owls often established residence in prairie-dog towns, and while the dog didn't think out the link, he felt instinctively that supper might be somewhere around. But a pile of dried manure brought him up short. He inhaled wheezingly, and water began to run from his nose. He opened his mouth and inhaled again, and then he had it. Mules! Most unmistakably, mules!

68

With the familiar scent came lightning flashes of memory, and with memory came sudden, deep longing for the companions last seen plunging up the bank of another dry arroyo with a wave of red water churning toward them. The dog stood up on his hind legs and sniffed a higher current of air, excited but not at all surprised. Having once smelled mule, he saw no reason why his own mules shouldn't be nearby.

Black Ears led him to the next pile of droppings. It was only a few yards away. Mules have so much fellow feeling that when one of their members decides to heed nature's call, the rest usually decide to follow suit, one after the other. The old dog had determined "mule," but the scent was so old that he couldn't be sure if it were that of his own mules. He whirled and snapped at Black Ears when she joyously rubbed first one side of her face, then the other in the droppings and prepared to roll on them. She docilely withdrew a couple of feet.

Whither the mules? The old dog circled, casting out farther and farther, seeking a trail. It was futile. To both north and south rose broken walls of low, reddish mesas, their tops dotted with the green of cedar and juniper. The dry riverbed and the train tracks here in the flats paralleled the mesas, heading northeast. The old dog stood whining softly, sorely troubled, and it was a relief when the female pricked her black-tipped ears and trotted a few feet ahead, looking back at him, urging him to angle with her back to the riverbed. The pack was apparently on the move again. The old dog knew intuitively that any animal moving between the mesas would stay near the water supply in the riverbed, and although he stayed on the bank while the pack stayed in the sandy bed, he allowed himself to be led along with them.

This journey was not long. Sunset dyed the western sky gold, apricot, and blood-red, and the red walls of the mesas were accumulating their first violet shadows when the old dog, from his route on the bank, sighted a land of plenty and gave the staccato bark that the pack used to signal game. Ahead lay another vast prairie-dog colony. It was far bigger than the last.

69

It stretched from mesa on the south to mesa on the north, easily ten miles across, and it was wider than his poor eyesight could pick out. But if he couldn't see stationary objects clearly, he could see movement, and he barked again as he suddenly noticed a coyote loping ostentatiously through one suburb of the rodent metropolis, deliberately serving as a focus for high-pitched yips of alarm, while a second coyote inched forward from a heavy clump of greasewood, aiming for a stealthy kill.

The dog pack came at a rush out of the riverbed, perhaps alarmed by the old dog's loud barking. Except for quick yaps, the wild dogs did no barking themselves. The two coyotes promptly loped away, through the acre upon acre of tail-flicking, alarm-yipping prairie dogs. In steady waves along the coyotes' path, prairie dogs scurried for their burrows as the coyotes approached, then popped out their heads and watched as the coyotes departed.

For a prairie-dog colony, this one's apparent vastness was really pretty meager. Where grass and weeds grew more abundantly, colonies twenty to thirty miles wide weren't unusual, and in Texas, to the despair of ranchers there, one stretched a hundred miles wide and two hundred and fifty miles long. But to the hungry pack, the colony looked like the promised land. They made quick work of dining. The prairie dogs were settling down for the night, and the grasses were eaten down to the bare ground in a huge circle around the colony, affording little cover except greasewood, but the prey was so plentiful that even two of the pups managed to catch their own banquets, and there was great growling and snapping and, in the end, plenty to share. They retired to the riverbed with full stomachs, and that night they enjoyed a singsong. They didn't deliberately sing from happiness. It just happened, after the night train went by, that the third female put her nose up to sniff the wind and emitted a short moan. The young dog decided to moan with her, long, lingering, high-pitched, and somewhere by the south mesa a mournful undulation suddenly

70

answered. Coyotes. As if to sing them down, the entire pack began to howl, and the great silence of the desert gave way to the eerie song of the canine, repeated and repeated again, sad, menacing, and utterly wild.

Only the old dog did not sing. The wind was from the north. He put up his nose with the others, but it was to smell. He couldn't tell for sure, but perhaps there was something on the wind.

He lingered one more day with the pack. They gave no indication of moving on. They had found a good place, albeit one already well populated with other predators, the rattlesnake, the coyote, perhaps the wolf. Unless the dogs were frightened away by some other dog pack or man, here they would remain. The few pools of water in the riverbed would soon dry, but tomorrow was not today. This high desert was not stingy with water. Snow fell in winter. Springs seeped from canyon walls. Diligent digging in this or other riverbeds sometimes produced water. In the broken land in back of the mesas, little streams sometimes ran. Since the prairie-dog colony lapped from mesa wall to mesa wall, the pack could choose from myriad potential dens and still be within easy striking distance of food. Meanwhile, there was the hospitable riverbed.

But all day, while the others hunted and napped, napped and hunted, the old dog restlessly paced the edges of the prairie-dog colony. He knew, without knowing how he knew, that grazing animals such as mules do not tarry where predators abound. Black Ears followed after him, seeming increasingly restless herself as he ignored signal after signal telling him that game was at his feet. Yet, they ate amply. When fatigue overtook them at the north edge of the colony, she followed him willingly into the mouth of a box canyon, and she only seemed puzzled when he curled up where he was instead of heading back the five or ten miles to the others. She collapsed next to him, belly up, all four paws flopping loosely in

71

the air. The chill of the desert night roused her once, and she rolled over closer to him and slept with her nose buried in the thick fur of his shoulder.

Before first light brought faint ghosts of color to the walls of the box canyon, dawn's imminence brought a silvery cascade of song from a canyon wren. At the sound, the old dog rose stiffly to his feet once again and tested the air. There was nothing, but he left the canyon, followed by Black Ears, and jogged to the north. He had awakened knowing what he was going to do. He was going to go north looking for both scent and water. Where he found both, he would find his mules.

Black Ears followed for a half mile before stopping. She looked back over her shoulder, saying plainly, as dogs can, "What about breakfast? What about the others?" The old dog scarcely paused but continued on, and she trotted after him. As the distance increased, so did her puzzlement. He steadily swung his nose back and forth, trying for scent, and she also sniffed eagerly, thinking he had scented something interesting that she had missed, and it was she who first located deer droppings at the mouth of another canyon. The dog hesitated, staring up the canyon. No shallow box, it seemed to cut deep through the first mesa, and the air at golden dawn brought the tang of a luxuriant growth of cedar. And aspen, finding enough water to grow somewhere in the depths of the canyon? Like a human noting the buzz of a bee or the squeak of two tree limbs rubbing together but dismissing them as insignificant, he noted, then eliminated, the vegetable smells from his consciousness, and he went back to sniff the deer droppings. There was no trace of mule, but his mind was already made up. The canyon led north; it had water in it somewhere and other grazing animals had passed this way. Any one of the three might have been enough. He turned up the canyon.

Again Black Ears followed, but this time only for a few yards. She turned back a few steps, then seemed beset by indecision. She swayed, now north toward the old dog, now south

72

toward the pack. If the old dog had looked back, she might have followed him. But he didn't. Animals simply part, rarely realizing they are parting, and they don't bother with good-bys. Smelling his way up the canyon, the dog didn't realize until he was on the other side of a pocket of spindly, close-growing aspen that the young female was no longer in back of him. The necessity of keeping with the pack was too strong for her, just as the necessity of finding his own companions, the mules, was too strong for him.

It had taken a lot of luck and a little logic simple enough for a dog to understand, but he picked up definite mule scent, definitely of his mules, in the second hour. Brush was plentiful. When the ground grew hot, he took the scent from twigs and branches they had brushed against, and the scent kept getting stronger. Excited, happy, he climbed to the head of the first canyon and down the next until there opened out before him a valley, at one end of which was a shallow, blue lake. No streams fed the lake. Perhaps springs bubbled up from its clear depths, or perhaps it had fallen from the skies, drop by drop, as rain water. Upon its surface rode a flock of wild ducks and another of wild geese, and in lush grass to one end grazed wild ponies. A handful of horses was scattered among them. They bore saddle marks. Runaways from somewhere. And a miracle arose from the mud: two huge, shaggy bison, mother and son, somehow strayed so far from the eastward prairies they had once inhabited in the millions and somehow having escaped the slaughter that had reduced their number to only a few pockets of survivors.

But the dog had no eye for miracles. He had eyes only for another unlikely trio—Old Jeb and Young Jeb and a strange black mule trailing the rotted remains of a harness, all grazing quietly in knee-high grass.

He flung himself toward them. Animals scattered every-where. The Jebs started to run too, but Old Jeb pulled up short and stared keenly at the running dog and stood his ground until the last moment, then stepped aside to let the dog

73

run past him. That was all right. Mules were like that. The dog dropped panting in the grass, tongue lolling out to the last quarter inch, grinning his doggy grin.

There was an exchange between the two reunited animals, silent, but perhaps all the more profound without the interference of mere words. Old Jeb ambled nearer, and finally he permitted himself a mule's matey greeting, leaning over to nibble the dog's shaggy haunch, before calmly resuming his grazing. The sun was hot. The dog was ready to rest. He squished through the mud in which the bison had been cooling themselves and lay down in the shallowest possible film of muddy water. After a while he lapped some of it, then contentedly watched Young Jeb and the strange mule drift hesitantly back to Old Jeb. The dog was so still that they began to graze, and a hatch of hungry tadpole shrimp came to nibble on him to see if he were edible, kissing his sides and toes. He relaxed into an almost physical unity with the tiny crustaceans, the warm water, the mud beneath.

The dog had done his job. Now he forgot that he had done it. Another job remained to be done, but he had no thought for it now. For the moment, there was an end to all striving, and he slid into the lost joy of the animal paradise.

74

Eight

CLEAN BOY instantly grew alert when his dog, Tsilkali, stopped and stiffened. The dog was not a pet. Like himself, Tsilkali was his mother's shepherd and general laborer. She owned nearly a hundred sheep, and Clean Boy himself owned nineteen. Being a careful woman, she kept two other dogs to help Clean Boy and Tsilkali tend them all. The boy's father liked her better than his other wives, and he had lately brought home a fourth dog for her, a small, long-coated, naturally obedient dog, the best dog of all with the sheep. But as Clean Boy watched Tsilkali and the other two long-legged brown dogs stare, growling, toward his father's cornfield, he concluded the new dog was of little worth as a watchdog. Even when Tsilkali and the other two dogs burst into furious barking and rushed down the rocky slope toward the wide, irregular field in which clumps of young corn were already turning yellow, the new dog continued following the sheep out to morning pasture.

Clean Boy was no cleaner and no dirtier than other Navajo children, but he had been born with lighter skin than the average, hence his nickname. Although he was twelve years old, he looked like a boy of nine or ten. He was the eldest of five children, and to feed five well would have taken a flock of three hundred sheep. At that, he was better nourished than most Navajo children. In the past generation, the "lords of the earth," as fearful settlers had called the Navajos, had lost orchards, cornfields, sheep, horses, hogans and, in many cases, their lives when the United States had decided the haughty

Navajos were too troublesome. It would take more than Clean Boy's lifetime for the flocks of sheep to multiply again.

But for all that he was small, Clean Boy was wiry and strong, and he was as bold as the strong, wiry brown dogs with whom he shared the responsibility for the flock. It took him only a moment to make up his mind. Tsilkali and the others were still barking madly, so Clean Boy left the sheep to the new dog and ran down the slope to confront the unknown danger.

It could be anything—prowling coyotes after the sheep, even wolves or bear. Sheepherding was a boring business, and although Clean Boy feared the idea of bear, he almost hoped for coyote. He had no weapon except stones, but neither coyotes nor bears could be killed anyway. That was *báhádzid,* tabooed. Without slowing pace, Clean Boy scooped up several stones as he ran. He was expert in their use at chasing away predators.

At the foot of the slope, the valley in which Clean Boy's family spent the summer months widened to present a spectacular rockscape. Two parallel rows of flat-topped cliffs soared skyward, the near row ending on the horizon in a vast red face that looked to Clean Boy like the giant stone face of a man or an animal. It was early morning, a sharp, tingling dawn that hinted of fall, and while the mesa on the west side was sunlit, the cornfield through which the dogs were running was still in deep shadow. At first Clean Boy couldn't see what they were barking at, but then the climbing sun struck red fire, and he saw, escaping from the ripening corn it had been eating, a magnificent red mule. Then, *chinde,* another, and a black mule running behind the reds, a broken halter strap dangling.

Loose stock was a chronic hazard to unfenced fields, and Clean Boy was proud of Tsilkali and the other dogs for chasing away the mules, but a second thought followed instantly on the first. That broken halter. And the pillagers were mules, seldom seen among his people. They were obviously strays, of

76

wonderful worth. Even more important to Clean Boy, the two red mules seemed to him very beautiful. How high they held their heads. What dainty hoofs, little bigger than deer's. With quick decision, he whistled piercingly, calling Tsilkali off, and when the dog was slow to obey he sent a small stone smatting against Tsilkali's rump, then another just in front of his nose to drive the lesson home.

He had no rope. Except for the dogs, he was alone. But he ran faster than he'd known he could, determined to circle the cornfield and cut off the mules.

Help came from an unexpected quarter. Apparently hearing Clean Boy's whistle, the new little dog left the sheep and came flying down the slope, and at a gesture from the boy he tore after the mules, circling, just as the boy had intended to do, to cut them off. Nearing them, the little dog dropped to his stomach, then, without need for command, darted in front of the lead mule and dropped again as the mule swerved a yard or two to the side.

They were at the edge of the cornfield. They would be trampling the scrawny, struggling stalks. Clean Boy kept running, Tsilkali and the others now at his heels, hoping to save the corn as well as capture the wonderful mules.

But from the opposite side of the field suddenly appeared a large, black-and-white dog with a bobtail, hackles bristling, coming straight to where the little sheep dog was still darting, dropping, slowly bunching and turning the mules. At the sight of the bobtail, the mules bolted. The bobtail swerved to meet them. Clean Boy grunted, startled. He wanted those mules. His hands still held two rocks. He threw, and the big, strange bobtailed dog whirled, snarling and biting at his shoulder, where the rock had hit sharply. Clean Boy threw again, scoring a hit over the bobtail's eye. Blood appeared. He called to Tsilkali, urging him to help, and from behind the boy a brown streak that was Tsilkali rushed to meet the bobtailed intruder.

The bobtail tried to run, following the mules, but Tsilkali was far the faster. He charged into the big bobtail, bowling him over, and as the bobtail scrambled to his feet, Tsilkali stood growling ominously. For a frozen moment, they stood stiffly beside one another, then Tsilkali reared. The bobtail made no further attempt to run. He reared simultaneously, chest meeting chest, and they crashed into a rolling, twisting heap, teeth snapping loudly. The next moment the dogs were up and facing one another again. The bobtail shook his head, trying to fling a trickle of blood from one eye. Both feinted and shifted, like wrestlers trying for a good hold.

The bobtail was old, Clean Boy saw. There was white hair around his muzzle and a subtle look of pale dullness in the depths of the glittering eyes that stared fixedly at Tsilkali. Clean Boy felt a surge of relief. Tsilkali was an eager fighter, but it was good to think the terrible-looking jaws of his opponent might contain only worn teeth. But the teeth were still worth fearing. Tsilkali lunged for the bobtail's forelegs, trying for a bone-breaking grip, and the bobtail leaped aside, then leaped back in a lightning movement, slashing a bloody gash in Tsilkali's shoulder before jumping aside again. Tsilkali yelped in pain and retreated a step, and the bobtail twisted and slashed him in the neck before once again jumping free. Down they went into another rolling, fighting tangle. Although Clean Boy stooped for more rocks, he could find no certain target. But suddenly there was another dog in the fight, the tiny new shepherd, teeth buried in the heavy shag of the bobtail's rump, and, as if taking heart, the other two dogs rushed in.

With four dogs against one, the fight was over quickly. Clean Boy made no effort to stop it, but urged his dogs on. The old dog snapped desperately, but the tiny sheep dog maintained what it apparently thought was a death hold on the bobtail's shag, and its trifling but stubborn weight was enough to throw the bobtail off balance each time he tried his slash-and-jump-back technique. Tsilkali finally got the hold he had been trying for high on the bobtail's foreleg, and the other dogs growled and scrambled, biting wherever they could, while the bobtail thrashed madly from side to side, trying to throw them off.

Dislodged, Tsilkali rose and feinted in preparation for another lunge, but the bobtail seemed to know he was beaten. Ears lowered, bobtail tucked tight, he rolled belly-up. The little sheep dog instantly let go his mouthful of hair. The other dogs stood over the bobtail stiffly, as if daring him to rise, but the bobtail made no effort to do so. The exposure of his cringing, vulnerable stomach and throat was the white flag, total surrender.

Now they would kill him, Clean Boy thought. But, instead, the tiny shepherd relieved himself. Then went back to work, chasing after the three mules. Clean Boy stared after him, his face blank, then looked back at Tsilkali, still growling and grumbling over the recumbent bobtail. But the fight seemed to have gone out of all of them. "Eh!" Clean Boy said. "And will you not finish your job?"

The beaten dog glanced at him with old, frightened eyes, then looked away, as a beaten dog must. At this slight motion of its head, all three brown dogs growled, but none went any nearer. Clean Boy snorted in disgust. There was obviously no more danger from the old dog. "Go," he told the brown dogs. He pointed with his chin toward the direction the tiny sheep dog had taken. "Go help."

They went, not very willingly. Clean Boy waited yet another moment and saw the old dog hesitatingly get his feet under him and glance back at the boy again, as if asking whether he would be allowed to crawl away. Should he stone the dog to death? It was strange, this lone, old dog, appearing at the same time and place as three wonderful mules. Clean Boy saw that the dog was wounded, on ear, side of face, where the stone had hit over his eye, many wounds over his body. Well, then, no need to stone him more. Wherever the dog came from, Clean Boy thought he knew where the dog wanted to go—somewhere off to die by himself, before the brown dogs or wolves or a coyote pack caught him and, as was their way with the old and hurt, speeded him to his dying. The thought suddenly made Clean Boy uncomfortable. He remembered that it was dangerous even to look at a dead animal, unless it had been killed for food. The dead, whether human or animal, became ghosts, and followed.

Clean Boy backed away. The old dog then began to crawl in another direction, away from the cornfield. Good. Let him go. As he himself must go, there to the flat beyond the cornfield, where the new little dog and Tsilkali seemed to be edging the mules back toward the spring, two miles from his mother's summer hogan, from which they hauled their water. Good, again. Together they would have a chance of herding the mules along an easy path to the sheep corral. It occurred to him that the sheep had been left without a single custodian, but if he were quick and the new dog clever, they could be back to the flock before the defeated warrior or any other trouble could possibly come to the sheep. And he would have for his very own the three wonderful mules.

The old dog was far from dead, but he was hurting. The worst pain was in the foreleg that the largest of his opponents had clamped between grinding teeth. He simply accepted the other pains, and by accepting them eased his suffering from them. But although the hide on his left foreleg was largely intact, the grinding pressure of the viselike jaws had bruised the leg to the bone they were attempting to break. The old dog couldn't put his weight on it, and it was on three paws only that he crept from the cornfield and crawled up a slope to the dubious shelter of a clump of scrub trees from which hungry sheep had cropped off all the lower foliage.

From his vantage point, the dog could see part of the cornfield on one side of the slope and, on the other, a little community consisting of a rough corral and several three-sided shelters made of untrimmed branches and roofed with juniper boughs. Small children played in the dirt beside the

80

shelters, and adults occasionally moved purposefully among them. The dog shrank back into the trees. He was still limping, and he looked at the bruised foreleg with bewilderment. He licked it, but it did no good. He began licking those of his other wounds that he could reach. An acrid smell hung about him again. When all four dogs had been upon him and he had realized he was losing the fight, he had known acute fear, and his anal glands had reacted accordingly, secreting their highly odoriferous fluid. The smell was not repulsive to the old dog, being his own, but it may have proved exceedingly so to the others. Tooth and claw were not an animal's only weapons.

If defeat had been victory, he would have forgotten the dog fight quickly. It would have been done. But the beating humiliated and depressed him. On top of that he was anxious about the mules, both the Jebs and the new black, which he had accepted upon first encounter as part of his burden. He couldn't count, but he had known very well that his unlikely herd contained a new animal, and he'd been running his stiff old legs off teaching the new mule to move in a generally northern direction since harrying them away from the rain-water lake over a week before.

Now a human and four dogs had forced the old, urgent question back on him: Where were his mules? He watched the other humans down the slope with a deep suspicion new to him in his long dealings with people. His drooping bobtail perked up a bit the second he saw the mules, coming at a trot over the eastern rim of the broken valley in which the Indians made their summer home. The Navajo boy and the little sheep dog were herding them, and a man detached himself from the people below and ran to meet them. Two girls ran out halfway, followed by a woman. At a gesture from the man, the girls jogged onward to help funnel the mules into the sheep corral. The boy paused and spoke with the woman.

The old dog rose, trembling eagerly, unable to hear or smell much from his distance, but at his first step his left foreleg

81

hurt, and he dropped to his stomach again. Two other women hurried to the corral and helped secure the mules. There was much excited talking and gesturing, not with hands but with head movements. One of the women leaned to pat the little dog.

The old dog backed deeper into the clump of trees, growling. He was afraid of these people, and even of the little dog. He would wait and lick his wounds until no people or dogs were around, and then he would go to his mules.

The wait was long. In the evening, Clean Boy's uncle came on horseback with a friend, and everyone had to inspect and admire the boy's prize all over again. They took the mules from the rickety corral but haltered them securely with rope halters and hobbled them and tied them to the posts of one of the shelters. The hobbles and ropes were meaningless to the old dog up on the slope, but one of the younger children brought the sheep in for the evening, and the sight and smell of the three big brown dogs following the children was profoundly meaningful to him. Blue smoke began to drift upward from a fire of piñon twigs, and soon the smell of coffee boiling and bread frying filled the air. Long strings of saliva dripped from the old dog's mouth all the time the people were eating. He stopped drooling only after the dogs had been fed and no smell of food remained. The little sheep dog returned after his supper to the flock. He had been raised with sheep since early puppyhood, given a bed of wool in the sheep corral and coaxed to suckle an indignant ewe, and he regarded sheep, not other dogs or people, as his natural intimates. After the fire went out and the soft voices fell silent, the brown dogs bedded down in a furry tangle between two of the shelters, too near the mules, too near, and the old dog continued to wait. The wind changed in the night. They caught his scent and set up a din of barking, and he had to creep down the other side of the slope and wait in the cornfield. The night lasted an eternity.

82

For Clean Boy, the night was long also. He awakened over and over, thinking about the beautiful red mules and the less beautiful but equally valuable black mule that he, a boy of only twelve, now owned. There was no question of his mother or his father claiming possession of them. Navajos regarded their children from birth as individuals with the right to own property and make independent decisions, so the only question about the mules was what to do with them. His uncle favored taking them all the way to Albuquerque and selling them. He had traded horses there from time to time and knew people who would handle them without indulging in the Navajo's fondness for gossip. Mexicans owned mules. Whites owned mules. Someone might come looking for them, even the soldiers of American Chief at Fort Defiance. American Chief owned mules.

Clean Boy knew he would probably follow his uncle's advice, but he sighed at the thought of giving up the red mules. He had no horse of his own. His father said he was still too young to need one. Why, he could ride the beautiful, quiet mule and lead the beautiful, nervous one, and once the mules had been fed back to fatness and their coats well curried, those red coats would shine like a reflection of the sun against the deep red rocks with which his country abounded. Everyone would admire the mules—and, Clean Boy conceded to himself proudly, they would also admire him. How beautiful, he thought, falling asleep. He awoke to see that the stars, blazing through the juniper boughs above his blanket, had barely moved, and it was still hours until morning.

Then when it was morning he overslept. They always arose before sunup. His mother sent his littlest sister to pinch him, and she laughed at him as he staggered to the fire and waited for a coffee cup to be emptied by one of the adults so he could drink the rewarmed brew. Clean Boy laughed back sheepishly, but he knew that his mother regarded her family's newfound wealth very favorably. Coffee both last night and this morning. What splendid extravagance. His people had acquired an avid taste for coffee in the bad time when they had been dependent on the largess of American Chief as exiles at Fort Sumner, but coffee had to be bought at the trader's, and it was expensive. Clean Boy drank, his eyes all the time trained through the thinning darkness to the scuffing sounds that told him the mules were moving about as well as their tie ropes and hobbles would allow them, no doubt looking for forage.

"Eh, nephew, shall I water your livestock while you are away this morning with the sheep?" his uncle teased.

Clean Boy hoped, at least, that he was teasing. He was jubilant when his mother said his eight- and ten-year-old sisters could take the sheep out that morning. His father frowned a little at her decision, but Clean Boy's mother said tartly that the new little sheep dog he had brought her had well proved its worth and could probably be trusted with the sheep all by itself. His father's other two wives, both sisters to his mother, agreed with her, and his father said no more. Instead of finishing the new silver bridle trappings he had been making, he began sharpening his hoe, a short-handled, large-bladed affair, so Clean Boy knew he was going to the cornfield. It was a clean field, with few weeds, and his father worked hard on it. Ordinarily, Clean Boy would have hoped to accompany him, but today he leaped to help his uncle and the uncle's friend trail their horses, hobbled but allowed to roam during the night, so they could take all the animals to water at one time.

The two miles to Owl Spring never went so quickly. Clean Boy rode double on his uncle's horse, staring proudly back at the three mules trailing behind on lead ropes. Once the mules smelled water, they trotted and caught up. Perhaps he should have watered them last evening, but he had been afraid they might escape the dogs and he would lose them.

His uncle put no reliance in the new mules either. He turned his horse loose with a slap on the rump to send it on to the spring, and his friend did the same, but they kept the less trustworthy mules on the ropes and led them into a shallow defile, little larger than a house. On its rim, nothing grew. But on the

84

floor of the defile, ten feet down, another world existed in miniature. Maidenhair fern, dewed with moisture, raised trembling, deceptively fragile-looking fronds over a luxurious mat of velvety moss in which water-filled hoof- and pawprints had been left. At their marshy edge, bright grass began, following a thread of water which trickled from the spring pond and into a series of small pools twenty, thirty feet downhill, and disappeared into thinner grass. Then the grass ended, and the sandy soil was bare, except for a crosshatch of delicate footprints, showing the steady traffic of birds, lizards, insects to the waters of the spring. The horses were drinking deeply by the time Clean Boy and the two men arrived at the defile, each leading a mule, but, as if disturbed, the horses raised their heads and left the water. The mules, too, pricked long ears toward a lip of rock directly atop the spring. Without warning, the horses broke into a run, almost colliding with the mules and men at the mouth of the defile.

"Hie!" shouted the uncle's friend. "What's gotten into them?"

Clean Boy's uncle wasted no time shouting, but threw all three mules' lead ropes to Clean Boy and ran after the runaway horses, his friend chasing behind. The mules plunged and reared and bumped into each other, and Clean Boy had to fight hard to keep his grip on the ropes. Even when they settled down to mere head tossing and ferocious displays of their long yellow teeth, they showed no interest in the water for which they earlier had appeared so avid. Clean Boy coaxed and pulled and finally backed into the spring pond, trying to drag them to its edge. Surely, once they discovered the water, they would remember their thirst. It was good water.

The water was also cold, and so was the morning. Standing knee-deep in the spring pond, Clean Boy heard his teeth begin to chatter. But he heard another sound that drained all feeling from his body. Directly over him rocks clicked, and one of the red mules let out a loud snort. Clean Boy started to turn his head, but a low, deep growling stopped him.

He knew instantly what animal it was. It was the dead dog, the bobtail, that he had let his own dogs kill. It never once occurred to Clean Boy that the dogs had not mortally wounded it. His suspicions of yesterday were correct. Dead, it had turned into a ghost. Or, horribly worse, it was a human wolf, such as witches turned themselves into, and Clean Boy's only uncertainty was whether a dog's form or something even more ghastly stood growling on the rock over his head.

He was afraid to look, but he had to. The growling intensified as the boy's head slowly turned. It was no mere dog that he saw, no, a witch, planted tensely above his head, swaying back and forth almost imperceptibly to build momentum to spring. The witch's lips were curled back so far that they appeared as only a dark border for the great, threatening teeth.

Clean Boy never felt the ropes drop from his hands. He never saw the mules mill for an instant, then spurt out of the defile. He stood frozen, staring at the witch, and then he blinked and the witch was gone and silence washed in to replace the vicious snarling. He sank to his knees in the icy water and didn't feel it, and he was still there when anxious arms grasped him and lifted him from the spring and patted him and felt him and an anxious voice kept saying something, and another voice said something about ". . . mules? Go after them?"

At that, Clean Boy roused himself. "No, no," he said, "they went with the witch. My uncle, help me. Will I die?"

"Witch?" said the uncle's friend. He looked around fearfully. It was full daylight and witches roamed by night, but one could never be too careful.

The tracks left by three mules, all trailing lead ropes, were clear, but neither of the men made any effort to follow them. They helped the boy onto one of the horses and left instantly. For as soon as the boy had pointed it out, they could see clearly that a witch had indeed taken the mules—a three-legged witch, from the set of the great pawprints impressed in the moss, slowly filling with water, and for all they knew three-headed as well. Good riddance to mules that were guarded by a witch.

Nine

THE WOUND over the old dog's eye infected and the eye swelled. The bone-bruise in his injured leg remained painful to walk upon. His pace was so slow after his encounter with the Indian dogs that the mules had ample time to graze, and they put on a little flesh to pad their protruding ribs. Grass was in good supply until they came down from the last red mesa and passed through a barren, badly eroded stretch that seemed to be having its first rain in a decade. Little grew, not even sage. Almost every afternoon, a gray, drizzling rain fell, simple misery for the animals, but soon the rain obscured richer, sage-dotted country, and then they entered an area where grass sprang up vigorously again. With painful slowness, the high desert approached the low and lazy toes of the massive mountain chain that stretches intermittently from the Arctic Circle to Cape Horn, the strong backbone of the Western Hemisphere, the land of the eagles.

One day when the peaks of the Rockies were still as hazy and indistinct as clouds, the dog came to a river. He had been terrified of running water since the flood, and he couldn't bring himself to try to swim it. Their direction for some days had been almost due north, but now he turned northeast again and followed the river, although at a respectful distance, vainly seeking a way to cross. His chance finally came at a toll bridge built to serve supply wagons en route to the rich San Juan mining area to the north across the Colorado line. The bridgekeeper awoke on a gray, rainy dawn to hear the hollow echo of hoofbeats clattering across his bridge and he turned over, cursing all bandits and thieves who would use a man's property without paying for it. He didn't see the animals. The next person who did was Angus M'Taggart, who chanced upon them in a meadow not far from his cabin in a mountain range named La Plata, thirty-seven wild miles from Durango.

In Durango, they called Angus M'Taggart "the hermit" or sometimes "the miser," but in reality he was neither, for he was beset with neither an overpowering greed for solitude nor for gold. He simply loved mountains—a legacy, along with his bony face, and his name, from his Scots immigrant father. Loving mountains, M'Taggart saw no reason why he shouldn't live in them if he so pleased. He was a tall, lean man, with long, lean legs that carried him along the mountain trails at a pace of twenty to thirty miles a day, if there was something he wanted to do that warranted his walking twenty or thirty miles. He enjoyed walking, but his pleasure on the rainy afternoon that he encountered the travelers was marred by a sight he had just gone to see. One of the many small cliff dwellings scattered across this southwest corner of Colorado had lately been visited by a party of curio seekers from back East, he had been told in Durango. M'Taggart had found them not only still camped at the site and using the ruin's roof beams for firewood, but hard at work with giant powder to break down walls, just to let in light. He'd sent a volley of rifle shots whizzing all around them. Let them think that over. Maybe he'd even go back in a couple of days and do it again if the party was still there.

M'Taggart didn't in the least object to their digging over the ruin in search of pottery and rotted baskets. He didn't even object to their blasting out the walls. To his mind, there were plenty of ruins and plenty of old pottery all over the place. As M'Taggart was well aware, a rancher was digging up a really big ruin on his place not far west on Mesa Verde, and M'Taggart didn't care a bit. What he did object to, however, was the mess that the Easterners were making, littering the ground with food cans and bottles, paper and twine, dropped and

90

broken pottery, not to mention crumbling bones and debris from their blasting. M'Taggart liked to keep his mountains neat.

The mountains were particularly beautiful this afternoon, turned a shimmering silver by the light rain. The peaks were lost in solid clouds, and M'Taggart knew that when the rain stopped, every valley would be filled with swirling fog. But the rain didn't stop. Cooler air rolled toward him, and he realized that a fresh downpour was coming his way. M'Taggart hastened his pace. He was near a stand of huge, thick pines that encircled a meadow. He would take shelter under them.

He moved quietly. It was habit. So when he chose his tree and crawled into the dry needles under its low-growing branches, he didn't disturb the two mules that he suddenly noticed in the meadow. One was black and one was red, and they were standing nose to tail, gently nibbling one another along the crest of the neck. Another red mule grazed a few yards away. The afternoon light all but disappeared in the silvery drizzle, but M'Taggart raised wildly unkempt eyebrows upon seeing an equally unkempt dog lying in the partial shelter of another tree, licking a front paw. The other paw was curled up under him, and the dog lay awkwardly on his chest, looking extremely uncomfortable. It took M'Taggart a moment to make out why. Then the dog turned his head slightly, and M'Taggart saw the swollen eye. He grunted, and the dog's good eye turned his way. The animal stiffened.

Before either could move, the rain struck hard. The comfort-conscious mules promptly crowded together next to the trees. Despite an all-encompassing odor of wet pine resin, one red mule smelled M'Taggart, but M'Taggart didn't move and the rain was coming down like a river, and the mule apparently opted to stay where he was, stamping and blinking futilely to try to dislodge a plague of mosquitoes that were competing with innumerable gnats for feeding space around his fetlocks and eyes. The dog, similarly gnat- and mosquito-plagued, slunk out into the downpour, favoring one leg, but

91

when the mules didn't follow he came back to a tree and stood indecisively. M'Taggart still didn't move. Soon the dog crawled a little way under the tree and lay there shivering, nose tucked between his paws.

M'Taggart had invested his emotions in soaring granite, and he had no soft feelings for pets. Dogs were no good if you liked to go places. You always had to worry about taking them with you when you wanted to shoot a deer or prospect a little, either that or walk ten or twenty miles back home to feed them. Then, they barked. And a man always had to be cleaning up dog dung. A cat, now, it would bury its messes tidily, but when people said cats were independent, M'Taggart had to laugh. They were always mewing around for food. They couldn't begin to go for a little five-mile stroll with you, for they were good for only a few spurts of running and couldn't possibly keep up with a man's steady pace. Besides, coyotes or wolves always got them. M'Taggart did once have a horse, and he cared for it well, but he never felt easy about it. It was a wild creature, unwilling prisoner to man, as all horses were, and to deny it freedom was a source of constant worry to him.

But this dog was so gaunt, and his thick coat was a solid mat of snarl and burr. And that eye. Poor fellow. Although M'Taggart didn't do it out of sentiment, he had set more than one broken bird wing and released so many growling, thankless animals from traps that Willy Benedict over near Parrot City once shot M'Taggart in the thigh to warn him away from his trap lines. M'Taggart held no rancor toward Benedict. He would have done the same. But he didn't stay away from the traps. The animals belonged to his mountains.

After a bit, M'Taggart spoke to the mules. They milled a little but stayed in their shelter. Progress. Not that it mattered to a mule, since M'Taggart had always understood they couldn't breed, but he noticed that the two red mules were male and the black was female. One of the red mules wore a frayed rope halter.

M'Taggart next tried speaking to the dog, and he was re-

92

warded by only a glance from the one good eye. The dog didn't growl, but neither did he make the slightest wagging motion of his bobbed tail. Too sick? Basically unfriendly? No, maybe worried that M'Taggart would make a grab for the mules.

While it had not occurred to the Navajo boy that the dog and the mules were traveling together, it never occurred to M'Taggart to doubt it, nor to doubt that they'd gotten lost and were trying to find their way home to a back porch, a mule lot, or maybe the cabin of some miner who liked dogs and worked mules. Looking more closely, M'Taggart saw that the mules' hoofs showed signs of hard traveling. They were worn unevenly, and the youngest red mule had a deep crack in the back left hoof that fair cried out for a file. A bad rope burn there on the black mule, too, as though the black had half-hanged herself tugging off a rope halter similar to the older red's, maybe snagged somewhere. Just like the animals in the traps and their chewed-off paws.

M'Taggart didn't really want to interfere, but it was obvious these animals, too, needed help. Though the rain showed no signs of slackening, he crawled out from under his tree, very slowly and carefully, and approached the mules with all the velocity of an overfed inchworm. The heavy rain helped immeasurably. Already damp and cold, the animals were reluctant to bolt out into it, and the trees against which they huddled were too thick to push through. M'Taggart himself got soaked through all four of the flannel shirts and two pairs of German worsted trousers that were his customary summer wear. His feet already had been wet from walking in wet grass. Under his wide-brimmed hat, only his head was dry, and the hat soaked through and his hair was turning damp by the time he got one hand firmly on the halter worn by the older red mule. The injured dog growled warningly, but M'Taggart ignored him. After a moment, the dog slunk a few feet farther away.

Then, thank goodness, a man could move briskly and get

home out of this rain. M'Taggart led the one mule and the two others followed, as he thought they would. The dog sneaked silently after them, so wolflike that although M'Taggart resolutely kept his face toward the twisting game path that he followed, he felt very uneasy right between his shoulder blades.

Then he was over a ridge and up a hogback and on the rim of a shallow bowl, and there on the far side was the roof of his cabin. No smoke came from the stovepipe, but to M'Taggart it looked delightfully cozy. A shed with an enclosure of aspen posts leaned beside the cabin. His horse had once lived there. It would be a tight fit for three big mules but better than staying out in cold rain. He led the roped mule inside the enclosure and waited patiently for the two other mules to decide to enter, and then discovered that he had apparently burned the rickety gate for firewood after the horse had died of lockjaw, and he had to jury-rig a new gate out of the wooden sledge that he used to drag home logs. The dog could slip through the gaps in the aspen posts.

The next problem was what to feed the animals. Inside his cabin, M'Taggart's eyes fell on a fifty-pound sack of oatmeal that he had carried on his shoulder the entire thirty-seven miles from Durango, and he sighed. Next to mountains, M'Taggart loved oatmeal. He had plenty of venison. A pity the mules couldn't share that with the dog, but the dog would settle down quicker if the mules were eating and contented. When the weather cleared, he would cut the mules a few armloads of wild hay. Meanwhile, he sighed again and found an old bucket and relayed out both raw venison and dried oatmeal to his guests. The dog was nowhere in sight, but M'Taggart wasn't worried. Where the mules were, the dog would hang around. Maybe tomorrow, maybe the next day, the dog might even let him look at that eye.

Now M'Taggart sighed with contentment and lit a fire. He was torn between venison and oatmeal for his own dinner, and he settled for a stew of the former thickened with the latter. If he'd only had an onion, he decided later, toasting his bare toes

94

while his socks dried, it would have been downright good. Next time he went for a five- or fifty-mile jaunt in his mountains, he'd keep an eye out for late-growing wild onions. Maybe the next time he walked into Durango for supplies, he'd even buy a tame one.

M'Taggart's oatmeal supply dwindled rapidly, and he saw that he would have to make the trip into Durango far sooner than he'd expected. The three mules liked oatmeal dry and they loved it cooked, slurping it delicately with a twisting motion of their mobile upper lips, as though savoring every mouthful. M'Taggart gathered them plenty of hay, but they still looked forward to oatmeal, and the black mule nickered like a horse every time she saw M'Taggart come out the door of his cabin. Her penchant for oatmeal both exasperated M'Taggart and endeared her to him, and he took to calling her Margaret after a younger sister whom he hadn't seen for twenty years or more. He didn't name the other animals. One red mule seemed aloof and the other skittish, especially when M'Taggart got out his file and smoothed their ragged hoofs, and the dog gave no signs of ever coming around. It was all right. The venison disappeared each day, and M'Taggart knew that each double handful of the raw meat in the dog's belly would start him back toward health as well as any medicine. M'Taggart also suspected he was helping the mules with the oatmeal. Showed he had good sense. The big-shouldered, big-footed dog hung around the shed, apparently sleeping in with the mules at night, and he stopped going far when the bucket with the oatmeal came out the door. Then the hour finally came when, panting nervously, he stood trembling next to the shed and let M'Taggart treat his eye, staring ahead with resignation out of the good one.

It was a nasty wound. Some sort of foreign matter down deep in, curled hair or dirt or something.

"What'd you do to yourself, then?" M'Taggart murmured quietly as he felt around it. "Let a foxtail work its way in?

Grass with those spiky things, that's worse than cactus. I guess you know we got to get it out. You just hold still now."

The surgery was accomplished with M'Taggart's pocket-knife. The dog flinched but he didn't wriggle or whimper, and M'Taggart regarded him admiringly.

"Taken like a man," he said. "Now let's have a look at that paw you keep favoring. Hmm. Nothing wrong that I can see, except you've worn all your pads just about off. Well, I've got you a surprise I've been cooking up. Made you some moccasins. Real deerskin, just like an Injun's. Hold still, now. We'll just rub those pads good with grease. . . . That's good, that's fine. Sheep dogs where my people came from, they used to make them boots of the prettiest yellow leather. They wore their pads down like you, so many rocks. No, all right, there's nothing to start squirming about. We've got to tie them on. Well, for the love of Mike, you can stand still when I'm gouging you with a knife, but you can't stand still for . . . All right, darn you, but you look like a darn fool wearing three boots and one foot bare!"

The next day, the leather bags M'Taggart had stitched so carefully to protect the dog's cracked and broken pads were gone. The dog looked guiltily at M'Taggart when he came out with the morning oatmeal, and for the first and last time there was a faint, guilty wigwag of his tail. M'Taggart concluded the dog had eaten the moccasins. He was disgusted, but more with himself for fooling with them than with the dog. At least the dog now seemed in a docile mood. M'Taggart took advantage of it by working his coat over with the late horse's curry comb, to try to remove what he could of burrs and barbs before they could work their way into the flesh. What there was of it. M'Taggart put down the curry comb shaking his head. Under all that shag, the dog was little but bones supporting a distinct potbelly, product of the venison and oatmeal he had lately been eating. M'Taggart decided he'd better shoot another

96

deer. Maybe a couple. This fellow could eat that much, and benefit from it, before the meat spoiled.

He took down his rifle that same afternoon, meaning to check a few draws where he had seen deer traces recently and be in good position to pop one off by the time evening came and game started moving. When he went out of his cabin he found all three mules standing in back of the wooden sledge he'd rigged as a gate, tossing their heads and watching the dog, who was nosing around in front of it. Instead of shrinking away, the dog came to M'Taggart and nudged him in the leg, as if in apology for something. Once again, in the way the dog carried his bobtail and lowered his ears, there was a guilty air about him. The mules seemed unusually restless. Wolves? They came around sometimes.

But, no, it was something else. M'Taggart stopped and studied the animals. "What is it?" he said to the dog. The dog ducked his head and glanced up at him. With both eyes. The sore still hadn't completely healed over the bad eye, but the swelling had gone. The dog moved a few feet away and sat in a patch of sunlight, and his tongue lolled out, and he didn't seem to want to look at M'Taggart except sideways.

"Oh ho," said M'Taggart. "Caught you in the act, did I? What'd you have in mind? Breaking these oatmeal-eaters out? I'll tell you, dog, you get a little more meat on you and that eye and those paws get all well, and I won't make you stay unless you want to. But you're in no shape for traveling on now. I'll tell you something else—if you've got good sense you'll stay around till spring. Don't you know what the wind's saying? Aspens'll start yellowing any day now. Real high, they're already orange. And high, it won't be any time till we're getting snow."

Only the black mule appeared to be listening. She craned her neck between two of the close-set aspen poles as if looking for M'Taggart's feed bucket, then stamped and raised her head and waved her upper lip in the air. Like the dog, both red mules looked carefully away from M'Taggart, and he tight-

97

ened his lips in exasperation. "One good push and you'd have had that old sledge down any time you wanted to," he told them. "Don't you go reckoning on me to open it for you."

M'Taggart had far less ability to understand the animals' simple but effective language than even the dog and the mules had in communicating with one another, but there was unmistakably something expectant, something urgent, in the way the foursome was acting. Did they really want to be free, or was he imagining it? Just because he demanded freedom for himself didn't mean that dumb animals were hoping for it, or that they should be allowed what they hoped for. It would be unforgivable of him not to act in their best interests.

A little ripple of wind set the wild grasses dancing around M'Taggart's cabin, and in a tall pine a jay screeched and flew, a bright blue flash against a bright blue sky. "Well, heck," said M'Taggart, and he lifted the heavy sledge away from the entrance to the mules' prison. "Maybe you're just tired of oatmeal and want some fresh grass. You'd better still be here when I get home."

But they weren't. There was no sign at all of the old dog and the three mules when M'Taggart returned shortly after nightfall, knees sagging under the weight of a young buck slung across his shoulder. M'Taggart decided it was just as well, for he'd often thought of using the shed to hang game instead of smelling up his cabin with it, and this buck was so fresh it would have to bleed awhile anyway. But as he lit his fire and sat beside it to take off his boots, he was surprised at how quiet it was. No stamp, stamp, of three greedy mules waiting outside in the shed. No snuffling sounds, and sometimes snores, from some old dog. M'Taggart laughed a little at himself, but not happily. In all the wild solitude of his jostling, thrusting mountains, he had never before felt lonely.

98

Ten

WITH THE EXCEPTION of the black mule, the animals thought no more about the man once they left his premises, and they left as soon as his back disappeared over the rim of the bowl in which he had built his cabin. It was not time to wait around. The dog could not see the mighty wall of mountains that lay in their path, but he could feel some vast presence, from the way the wind blew and the sun fell and the cold flowed over the skin of the land. Nor was the old dog immune to the message of the wind. And although he saw the world only in shades of gray—light and dark instead of color—he didn't need to see green aspen leaf turn butter-yellow to know that cold can come early in high mountains. He could hear. The rustle of the leaves had a papery sound as they began to dry. Tree limbs seemed to creak and groan more loudly. The air had a snap, and a different smell. It was time to go. The man had sheltered and fed them, but the deep, unsatisfied yearning that his reunion with the mules had reawakened in the dog said go, so he herded them out of the enclosure with no vacillation whatever. Just to be safe from interference, he set off in the opposite direction from M'Taggart.

Things were different with the new mule that M'Taggart had named Margaret. She'd liked the man who had kept her so well supplied with oatmeal. He was the first human she'd seen at close range since running away from her owner, and he made her think more tolerantly of all humans, with the exception of the still-remembered daughter of her former owner, who, by earning Margaret's disapproval, had led to her life of vagabondage. The child had offered a fistful of carrots to her father's new mule, then had been cross when Margaret sniffed the new fodder cautiously instead of bolting it down. So she threw the carrots in Margaret's face, with predictable results. Margaret got a beating, and she didn't forget it. Like all mules, she wouldn't stand for abuse. She thought about it for two full years of plowing in her owner's beanfields, and one morning as she was being led to the plow she bit the man firmly on the shoulder and departed. But M'Taggart had in no way offended her. She kept turning, thinking of the man and his oatmeal, and the dog kept heading her back. Finally, she apparently forgot and fell in behind the Jebs. They were able to make progress until rough ground and the pitch-black shadows cast by heavy timber made Old Jeb decide he'd had enough for one night.

In the dawn, a low fog left moisture trembling from every leaf under which they passed. The animals were damp. They were chilled. The dog moved painfully until the sun warmed him and his stiff joints loosened up. They neared a winding dirt road, and he regarded it cautiously. It was going east, but a little southeast. Besides, although one man had been kind to them, a road was an ominous indication that somewhere nearby might be a whole colony of those creatures they had learned to avoid, men.

Then came a scent that sent him whining and scampering like a three-month-old pup. His outburst startled the wits out of Margaret. The two Jebs, however, both came and sniffed with great interest at a trailing mat of bearberry that edged the road. To it clung a reeking odor of pyroxylin and alcohol, of potassium iodide and nitrate of silver, of pyrogallic acid and potassium cyanide—the stench of a traveling photographer's wagon.

Because of the fog that had made them so uncomfortable, it was an ideal morning for following their noses. Trees grew on either side of the road, creating a tunnel down which a mild breeze breathed the yearned-for odor that clung to every twig.

The road no longer seemed ominous. Now it was the pathway to joy. Bobtail high and nose low, in his best tracking form, the old dog ran eagerly into the road, dashing from side to side, as though the scent was edible and he was frantic to gobble every morsel. He forgot his stiffness. He still favored his lame foreleg, and, except for his potbelly, he was still as gaunt as a starving wolf, but all the pain and bewildered misery of the past weeks also dropped away into splinters of memory that would come to him again only in whimpering dreams. Somewhere ahead was the familiar wagon. Home!

The dog also quite forgot another essential ingredient, the red mules. But the Jebs tagged behind scarcely less eagerly, drawing in the strong scent with a great quivering of wide, black nostrils. Margaret stuck with them, sorely puzzled but determined not to be left alone. Old Jeb was as excited as the others, but he was not too excited to overlook something that dawned only later on the eager dog. There was something familiar about this particular dirt road.

That bridge over that mossy creek, there, just ahead. Hadn't he and Young Jeb pulled the wagon over that bridge before, its wheels bumping and slewing on the untrimmed logs? And around that turn, yes, there it was, a second fork of the same creek, and another bridge of untrimmed pine logs. Next . . . yes, a larger creek joined the road and flowed along beside it. The road would stretch on through rocky foothills until it reached one of the many towns in which Old Jeb had stood munching oats by the wagon for a day or three or four, while people came and went, and the dog napped under the front wheels of the wagon, and their own man climbed in and out of the square at the back of the wagon and the fumes of the chemicals he used came rolling out. It seemed as if it hadn't been too long ago when Old Jeb stood very still one morning while his harness was being put on him, and kept his end of the double tree exactly even with that of Young Jeb to show the young mule how it was done, and then he pulled the wagon along this very road to some other town.

101

Old Jeb liked the recollection of that. He far preferred a complete and comfortable sameness to his days to this business of getting wet and cold and sometimes hungry and always having the dog weaving around his heels. The certainty that his old, boring wagon and his own, boring man were ahead in this town was pleasing to him, and he pushed ahead and left the dog to pant along behind.

But they closed ranks when, hours later, they actually entered the town. To an outsider, Durango, Colorado, might have looked like a raw, rank settlement still clutched by the indifferent arms of nature, but to the animals it was intimidating in the enormity of its strange smells and bustling population. Durango was a prosperous new town. The tents and pine shacks of its early days had quickly given way to respectable brick, and even the meat market sported wallpaper and kept a stuffed elk in a corner next to the sides of beef, not only to remind customers that wild game could be had, but for the sake of the elk's glassy-eyed beauty. Once just a narrow, foothill-squeezed bend in the valley of the Animas River, Durango was a railroad town, a smelting town, a ranching town, and, underneath it all, a rowdy Saturday Night town. The brawling element distressed the business interests, who pointed to Durango's amenities. Durango had a four-story hotel with no less than its own three-story privy. Durango had the biggest smelter in all of the mountain range so rich that it was known as "the silver San Juan." Durango had a two-story, two-winged Denver & Rio Grande Railroad depot, from whence tough little narrow-gauge locomotives puffed two by two up to Silverton, passing through a horrific gorge by cleaving to a meager shelf blasted out of the face of sheer cliffs. Just an easy hop-skip, claimed the Durango inhabitants, but the trip took one locomotive to pull and the other to push, and few tourists to this "Switzerland of America," as the Silverton inhabitants would have it, ever had the courage to repeat the trip.

A string of freight mules stopped traffic at Main Avenue and Seventh Street by filing through, one by one, each drag-

102

ging two twelve-foot pine beams toward one of the mines, where they would be used to shore up a new tunnel. The mule skinner, riding his favorite mule at the head of the line, looked keenly at the two Jebs and Margaret as they darted past his string. Stray livestock was not uncommon, but the skinner knew most of the mules for a twenty-mile radius, and he'd never seen these before. He couldn't leave his charges, but he shouted at an acquaintance coming out of the Silver Moon Boarding House and exchanged a few words with him.

The acquaintance flapped hastily down Main Avenue after the strange mules, his ankle-length overcoat snapping behind him like a flag in high wind. His haste attracted attention. A man in a bowler and two more in miner's clothes turned to stare speculatively at the ownerless mules. The old dog, on the other hand, attracted the attention of a trio of town dogs, but these fled at the sight of a greater menace, a group of town boys who were no older than four or five, but who, having learned only the cruelty of the weak and not yet the common bond of pain, were already adept at tormenting their town's four-footed citizens.

The dog saw no one. For one thing, he was too busy trying to follow the all-important scent through all the confusion of stale beer, washed and unwashed bodies, sweating animals hauling passing wagons, garbage, new cloth, rotting filth under wooden sidewalks, and fresh paint. For another thing, eye-level for the dog was only a foot and a half from the ground, and he could see little but a forest of dangerous legs and wagon wheels all around him. But the scent got stronger and he burst into a run and dashed into a vacant lot next to a sign shop, where the odor of the fresh paint battled with that of pyroxylin and alcohol, of potassium iodide and nitrate of silver, of pyrogallic acid and potassium cyanide—at last, after all these weary miles, the precious wagon. In a paroxysm of barking, he ran to it, then all around it, then jumped up into the spring seat, still barking.

A woman screamed inside the wagon. The scream held

103

more anger than terror, but the dog himself was terrified. He jumped down and cowered away from the wagon. He was slow to realize that the sides of the wagon's enclosed area were canvas, not wood, and that the spring seat had bounced differently under his leaping paws. The scent was right. This *had* to be his wagon.

The Jebs thought so too. Not particularly put off by the woman's continued screaming, they sniffed around the wagon, succeeding in trampling the tent stakes of an unknown and therefore irrelevant white tent pitched next to the wagon. The tent ropes sagged and so did the tent. It collapsed slowly on Margaret, who didn't care for any of these goings-on and kicked, connecting with Young Jeb, who screamed and reared. A man's angry voice came toward the wagon, followed by other men's voices, and the dog suddenly knew the deep hurt and anger of the betrayed.

Where was his own man? He was supposed to be here, not these shouting strangers. One strange man grabbed at Young Jeb, and the dog went mad. He had never in his life attacked a human. They were gods. He had nerved himself to approach the Navajo boy who had taken his mules, and might actually have jumped him, but it hadn't come to that. Now he charged, into a swirl of flapping coattails, slashing viciously, trying for flesh and blood instead of cloth.

The men who had been pursuing the mules fell back. In the photographer's wagon, a woman's angry, frightened face popped through a gap in the canvas covering. Only the photographer kept coming, though timorously, to defend his wife and property. He was temporarily in the city of Durango to take most excellent pictures of its streets, stores, private buildings, and citizens, while on a view-taking tour of the grand, majestic, and picturesque San Juan Mountains. He would provide enlargements from pictures in any size in ink, crayon, pastel, or water color done in the very finest style. He was from Colorado Springs and his name was Victor L. Hoagland.

104

By the time Miss Agatha Hicks came down Eleventh Street and turned onto Main Avenue, a considerable crowd had gathered, but not a man in it had a gun. The fellows from the sign shop had run home to get one, for the obvious move was to shoot the snarling, slavering dog that was terrorizing the photographic artist's wife and keeping honest men from confiscating those three obviously ownerless mules. Meanwhile, it was correct to permit the little Townsend and Hamilton boys to throw rocks at the dog. Nor did it hurt to grab up a handful of rocks from the vacant lot in which the photographic artist had set up shop and help the little boys chunk the killer dog.

At least that's what Agatha instantly gathered that many of the men in the crowd seemed to think. One, Oscar Gard, merely reacted to cruelty with the same pleasure as the Townsend and Hamilton brats. Agatha aimed straight for Oscar, pushing her way through the crowd, her color high. She had known Oscar Gard since both were children in Central City, Colorado, and he had been mean even then. He especially hated cats and bragged that he never missed an opportunity to kill one. Agatha presently had a four-month-old kitten at home, Scraps, which would never be able to walk without dragging its hind legs, thanks to Oscar's having dropped it down a prospect hole and left it there to mew feebly for days until Agatha chanced to hear it.

As she neared the rock-throwing Oscar, Agatha saw that Mr. Victor L. Hoagland was using Oscar as a shield. Hoagland was edging toward the frantic dog with a stout stick of firewood held behind him. Agatha had disliked Hoagland for reasons of her own since he'd pulled into town a few days before, but she believed in being polite.

"Beg pardon," said Agatha, and she plucked the heavy stick from Hoagland's hands, swung it to her shoulder like a baseball bat and whammed Oscar as hard as she could against the back of his shoulders.

Oscar staggered and turned, fists clenched, but when he saw

105

Agatha he only inquired plaintively, "Now, Agatha, what'd you do that for?" Oscar remembered Agatha when she still tore into people with her fists instead of reaching for a weapon. A superior boy, later a man, could not, of course, hit back.

"I'll hit you again if you don't stop tormenting that dog," Agatha assured him. "You, Bert Townsend, you call off those two boys of yours, or I'll have a word to say to your wife."

Agatha Hicks was tall for a woman, all of five foot seven, and although she weighed only a meager one hundred and fifteen pounds, she packed a wallop even more intimidating than the one Oscar Gard had just received: her father had risen to the post of superintendent of Durango's leading industry, the huge San Juan & New York Mining Company smelter. Everyone but the man in the flapping overcoat shuffled and looked sheepish as she surveyed them scornfully. The man with the overcoat was far too occupied in trying to hang onto both trousers and his belt, which he'd succeeded in getting around Young Jeb's neck.

Agatha's eyes swung to the beleaguered animals, and she gasped, "Why, for pity's sake! Those are Calvin Fairchild's animals! Let go of Mr. Fairchild's mule, you swine!"

"But, lady," the man with the overcoat panted, "these mules don't belong to nobody. Finders keepers."

"You're a liar and a scoundrel," Agatha said. The men murmured at the boldness of her language, but Agatha ignored them. She took a hesitant step toward the cowering but still growling old dog. Was she wrong? This ragged, wild-eyed creature so thin that his coat hung on him like a man in a suit four sizes too large . . . She knelt to his level so she could get a good look at him and he at her. "Nemo?" she said wonderingly. "Is that you, Nemo?"

The dog didn't really respond, but he quieted. He let Agatha touch him gently, protesting only by silently wrinkling his lips. "Good boy," she said. "All right, you're going to be all right, boy."

106

She stood decisively. "I say this dog is named Nemo and he belongs to another photographic artist named Mr. Calvin Fairchild, who comes through here every so often from Salida. And I say those two bay mules are named Young Jeb and Old Jeb, and *they* belong to Mr. Calvin Fairchild of Salida, and anyone else who touches them is going to have to reckon with me. You there, Henry McCoy." She gestured to one of the co-owners of the sign shop, a thin, mustachioed young man in a paint-smattered vest holding a .30-30 deer rifle. "Mr. McCoy, Mr. Calvin Fairchild sets up his traveling studio in this very lot every time he comes through. Do you mean to tell me you've never noticed his two bay mules?"

McCoy looked interested and self-important. "Well, now, Mr. Fairchild'd be the young fellow with the harelip, wouldn't he? He sure does have two bay mules. Got a dawg, too, black-and-white like this one. I've seen him with them many a time."

"And you'll see him again," Agatha said. She added in an indignant burst, "Mr. Calvin Fairchild takes excellent care of all Durango's photographic needs, and we don't need strangers coming through here trying to cut in on his business." Then she was afraid she'd said too much. She clamped her mouth shut tightly and only opened it to say, "Oscar Gard, you get you three ropes and you slip them easy on those mules and you bring them straight home with me. Give me your belt. I'll take this poor old dog."

"Just a minute, lady," the man in the flapping overcoat protested. "Maybe these bays belong to your Mr. Whoever, and maybe they don't, but I ain't heard a word about this black mule, and finders keepers."

"Finders, my foot!" Agatha spat. She smoothed her corsets with an unconscious gesture, and their suffocating tightness suddenly reminded her she was no contentious schoolgirl, but a twenty-six-year-old spinster and was therefore supposed to act like a lady. "I shall wire Mr. Calvin Fairchild at Salida this very day and inquire into this matter of his animals. *All* of his animals. If the black mule is not his, he will surely say so."

107

"What if he's not home, Miss Hicks?" inquired the sign painter. "He's always traveling around, ain't he?"

"The postmaster in Salida always knows Mr. Fairchild's whereabouts when he's on tour," Agatha said.

The rival photographer, Mr. Victor L. Hoagland, nodded knowingly, but he said, "Animals strayed, Mr. Fairchild not with them—it makes you wonder, doesn't it? I'm familiar with Mr. Fairchild's work. The rougher some pretty place is to get to, that's the view you always see with Mr. Fairchild's name on it. I'd hate to think a fellow artist has got up in the mountains somewhere and got himself lost or stranded. They tell me there's fresh snow galore up on the Needles."

Agatha worried all the way home, leading the reluctant but tractable old dog ahead of Oscar and the three mules. It was terrible to think that something might have happened to Mr. Fairchild. That man! He was as shy as this old mutt was, and just about as ugly, and he never seemed to know that anyone could find him charming. Or if he knew, he was just like every other man she'd ever met, with never a glance to spare for a twenty-six-year-old spinster who was not only too tall and too thin but who was stuck with keeping house for her widowered daddy. No. He'd look shyly at some young and plumply pretty woman, and look away and sigh, and never see what was right there, hopeful, in front of him.

But Agatha couldn't resist rejoicing, even in the midst of her worrying. If Mr. Calvin Fairchild wasn't dead somewhere in the mountains, her wire would surely fetch him. He would come quickly for his animals. And he wouldn't be able to help looking this one time at their rescuer, one Miss Agatha Hicks.

Eleven

EXCEPT FOR THE WAR, Raleigh Hillman had never been farther away from home than New Orleans, but he'd always wanted to go traveling. So when his nephew, Calvin Fairchild, came down sick in East Texas and crept home to Louisiana to recover on his grandmother's cooking, Uncle Raleigh decided to volunteer to see the restored Calvin safely back to the far land of Colorado.

It had been obvious to all the Fairchilds that someone should go back to Colorado with Calvin. Even when he swore he was feeling fine and not having the bad headaches any more, he looked as pale as a toadstool and fragile as dandelion fluff. Besides, the Fairchilds never could seem to get it into their heads that just because Calvin couldn't talk straight didn't mean he couldn't think as well as anybody else. Most of the Fairchild clan seemed to find proof positive of their opinion in the fact that Calvin was so cast down about losing a dog and a couple of mules. Even after he'd finally resigned himself to their loss, he wouldn't accept Uncle Dawkins Fairchild's offer of two fine-haired Kentucky mules as replacements, and the Fairchilds all clucked and fussed about that. But they were always clucking and fussing about Calvin. Uncle Raleigh thought privately that was why his nephew had decided to live so far away in the first place.

Strictly speaking, Calvin was only a nephew-in-law to Raleigh Hillman, and not a blood nephew, and that seemed to worry the foolish Fairchilds when Uncle Raleigh first said he'd go. Uncle Raleigh had put a large, heavily booted foot down on their misgivings. He knew that if things weren't settled fast, his one blood Fairchild nephew, his dead sister's boy, would be clamoring to go instead, and him in law school. The nephew clamored anyhow, but Uncle Raleigh had his way.

So that was why Raleigh Hillman was in the vicinity of Salida, Colorado, awkwardly flaying the trout stream in front of Calvin's cabin on the hazy, golden day the animals were found in Durango. Calvin was a half mile away with his big camera when Rob, the postmaster, came clattering up the road on a horse, looking elated and waving a telegram. Uncle Raleigh put down his pole and wallowed out of the willows by the stream to attend to proper greetings. He was the size of a bear and tended toward shagginess, so there was an interval of mutual apologies, from Uncle Raleigh for so resembling a bear, and from Rob for being so startled. Then Uncle Raleigh ushered the visitor into Calvin's cabin and put on the coffee pot and went to find Calvin. He didn't inquire into the contents of the telegram, although he suspected Rob hadn't been able to resist reading it himself. From the look on this other young man's face, whatever news the telegram contained wasn't bad, and that was all that counted to Uncle Raleigh.

He puffed through a field of wild hay above the cabin. It was alive with scurrying mice busily storing away grass seed, and Uncle Raleigh made a mental note that if his nephew refused to get another dog, he at least should get a cat. Finding Calvin wasn't easy. The scamp was sitting completely still, his camera braced on a boulder in front of him while he awaited the coming of a herd of mule deer. Uncle Raleigh only spotted him by the reflection of sunlight on his belt buckle.

"Hey, nephew, come a-running," Uncle Raleigh called. "Young man named Rob Elford's at the cabin with a telegram, and it looks like good news. Reckon one of them fancy New York magazines has bought some more of your views?"

Calvin came denying the possibility, but Uncle Raleigh had heard from Calvin's own mouth that he'd shipped a bunch of Apache Indian stuff to *Frank Leslie's Illustrated Weekly*.

110

Calvin still walked shakily, and Uncle Raleigh had to restrain himself from taking the fifty-pound camera on his own shoulder. Under all that shyness, Calvin was an independent fellow.

Witness the log cabin he'd chosen. It shared a whole mountain with only a ten-man mining operation, and the mine itself was miles farther up. It was a good cabin, snug and windowless on the north, but with two nice south windows in the cozy front room with its big sleeping loft right next to the chimney, and both an east and a west window in the kitchen. The big blue photographer's wagon stood right outside the kitchen door, water pump handy to both, and on the other side of the cabin, looking pretty forlorn, was a roomy barn built for the mules. A grove of aspens gave summer shade. Uncle Raleigh found the mountains cool and sweet, and he thought his nephew-by-marriage had made a good choice.

At the cabin, Uncle Raleigh left Calvin to his guest and went into the kitchen to see to the coffee. He especially liked the kitchen. It was the biggest room in the cabin, and it looked even better to Uncle Raleigh's eyes since they'd dressed the rafters with the two home-smoked hams and the garland of homemade sausage old Miz Fairchild had insisted on sending home with Calvin. Uncle Raleigh poured the coffee and filled the sugar bowl to the brim, but before he could get through the door with it, Calvin appeared in front of him, paler than ever and his face tense.

"It's all right, son, we can fix it," Uncle Raleigh said, although he hadn't the slightest idea what could be the matter.

Then Calvin's maimed upper lip split in the biggest smile Uncle Raleigh had ever seen on his face, and Uncle Raleigh had to smile too, because the same big smile was on the face of Calvin's friend Rob Elford, peering over Calvin's shoulder.

"You bet we can, Uncle Raleigh," Calvin said after the usual sputtering start. "Nemo and the Jebs are alive and found, and I'm leaving on the next train for Durango! Reckon you could go with me?"

111

Uncle Raleigh hadn't the slightest idea where or what a Durango was, either. Some place in Mexico, wasn't it? But having seen part of the world, he had no objection to seeing more of it. "Let's pack," he said instantly. "I wouldn't miss it for anything."

In Angus M'Taggart's favorite saloon in Durango, there was whiskey in barrels in the back room, pickles on the bar, and, rather than the usual stuffed heads of grizzly or wolf, a stuffed house cat in a place of honor over the free-lunch counter. It was a large yellow cat, its fur looking rather as if the moths had been at it, and it sat upright on its haunches with front paws held out in front of it. M'Taggart found it mystifying, and since the saloon's fare had little to recommend it, the cat was the chief lure that always brought him there whenever he made the two-day hike into town for supplies.

The next morning, sooner than usual because of his oatmeal shortage, M'Taggart went by Judd's Grocery to place a mumbled order for supplies, paid for them in advance, then reported to the saloon to have breakfast and to stare at the cat. He never spoke to anyone, but he liked to listen to the barroom conversation. Snow had fallen on Wolf Creek Pass, he heard another early customer tell the proprietor, and he concluded it was just as well that he'd decided to come into town. If winter was coming early to the high passes, it would reach his own mountains soon, and a wise man laid in ample oatmeal for the winter.

M'Taggart didn't ask the other customer how much snow fell. He was self-effacing around strangers. If he had ever broken his reserve long enough to ask about the saloon's stuffed cat, for instance, he would have learned it had been a treasured pet of the proprietor's, who, upon the cat's death at the age of sixteen, had it stuffed as a means of perpetuating its memory. But today, as always, M'Taggart didn't ask. He drank silently and steadily for his usual two hours, then left,

left oblivious to the world around him. M'Taggart indulged the weakness only on his rare town days, and drunks were no uncommon sight in Durango, so the clerk at Judd's Grocery only marveled at his ability to stand up under the weight of the oatmeal sack when M'Taggart checked in to pick up his supplies.

By now M'Taggart began to feel maudlin. He missed the animals, and he especially missed Margaret. Margaret would have carried the oatmeal for him, and not just as an unwilling slave, but willingly, as a gentle companion. M'Taggart had deliberately simplified his life, throwing overboard the extra skillet, the unused spoon, responsibilities, even friends, but now he discovered that he missed the simple circumstance of being of great interest to another living creature, even a creature with her avid eyes on an oatmeal bucket.

Heading out of town, M'Taggart thought at first he was imagining things. He could have sworn he heard Margaret's horselike nicker as he staggered past an imposing gingerbread-trimmed house. He stopped and stared at the double lace curtains on the front windows as though he expected to see Margaret peering through them. M'Taggart knew this block. It was where the highfalutin people lived. He teetered around to an alley of spacious dimensions, yawning from the heavy sack of oatmeal on his back.

He found the mules in a carriage house which he instantly condemned as being airless and dark. Sodden tears ran down M'Taggart's cheeks, and they worsened when he saw the dog. The animal was tied in a stall all by himself on a short rope, no longer than four feet, an untouched food pan and a bowl of water nested in thick hay beside him. The dog was curled up in a small ball. He looked utterly miserable.

"Ah, you poor old fellow," crooned M'Taggart in a faint echo of his father's burr. "Now what have they gone and done to you? Taken you captive, all four, and you that loves freedom as much as me."

The dog growled as if he'd never seen M'Taggart before, and M'Taggart returned to the mules, hurt. The mules also were tied, for two placid horses occupied the only other stalls, and M'Taggart grew teary again. "Poor Margaret," he said. "Poor lass, and you that has to roll all the time in nice clean dirt to keep your coat to your liking. Won't they even let you outside to roll? Don't worry, lass. Angus M'Taggart's here."

He had to stash the oatmeal and his leather pouch stuffed with other supplies before he could untie the animals. In sliding the oatmeal sack from his shoulder he dropped it with such a thump that a man came running from the kitchen door of the house, wiping cake crumbs from his mouth. He was a Cornishman, as M'Taggart could tell from the moment he opened his mouth, and apparently the stableman, for the man bawled authoritatively, " 'Ere, man, what's thee hup to, bothering 'em 'orses!"

Given enough whiskey and a good enough cause, M'Taggart could forget shyness and speak to any man. "Botheration to you," he replied with dignity. "What are *you* up to, locking up my dog and my mules?"

"Thine, his they? Miss Agatha 'Icks'll 'ave something to say habout that. Touch 'em, and she'll 'ave thy 'ide."

"You tell your Agatha 'Icks to see Angus M'Taggart if she likes trouble. I'll give her plenty, stealing a man's mules. Now stand aside. I'm taking them with me."

"Thee'll not take 'em," the stableman blustered. "That hold dog's got sore feet and 'e hain't supposed to move hoff that 'ay."

But M'Taggart could tell the Cornishman's heart wasn't behind his threatening air. The man skipped to the horses' stalls and took a protective stand there, but he appeared to feel he had done his duty by the mules and the dog by blathering about someone named Agatha 'Icks. He wouldn't be the first horse lover to look down on mules.

114

M'Taggart fumbled with their ropes. The Cornishman was bellowing again, something about not letting the mules get into Miss 'Icks' hiris beds, and M'Taggart didn't object at all when the man threw open the alley door of the carriage house. He turned to the old dog, who was straining against his rope, whimpering as the mules filed out into the alley. The dog didn't bother to growl this time when M'Taggart kneeled to untie him. He charged out after the mules without a backward glance, and there was a sudden commotion, as if his haste had frightened the mules, and at the same moment a voice called from the house, "Jack? Jack! Miss says 'itch the 'orses to the Stan'ope. Hits near train time."

"Now thee's done hit!" said the Cornishman in belligerent satisfaction, and he ran hollering toward the house.

M'Taggart was bumfuzzled. Here in enemy territory sat his fifty-pound sack of oatmeal and the pouchful of salt and flour and coffee and one onion. But there down the alley ran the animals he had come to rescue, and they appeared to be running away as rapidly from him as from their captors. M'Taggart left the pouch but shouldered the huge sack of oatmeal, bait, he thought cunningly, to catch the mules, and staggered off after them. He made it only to the end of the alley before an enraged young woman neatly attired in a black silk dress but with her hair only half combed caught up with him.

"You fiend!" she screamed. "What have you done with them?"

"Uh—" said M'Taggart.

"Put down that ridiculous sack and go get them," she ordered. "Go get them this instant!"

"But—" said M'Taggart.

"I'll shoot you, you tosspot, if you've lost Calvin Fairchild's animals for me!"

And then Miss Agatha 'Icks, M'Taggart presumed, turned red with rage and swung a roundhouse right that missed M'Taggart's face but connected with his left ear. Slightly stunned and greatly horrified, M'Taggart staggered back

115

to avoid further assault, but he had forgotten the sack of oatmeal. Its weight shifted ponderously on his shoulder and tipped him backward. He dizzily fought for balance, but he could feel himself going, swimmingly, sickeningly, caught by a wave of nausea that tipped him still farther, he fell over with a great thud, and the last thing he remembered was being glad the oatmeal was under him, not on top of him.

The train bearing Calvin Fairchild and his uncle whistled again and again as it highballed up the valley of the Animas River. It was running late, whereas it should have been early. The engineer, a dutiful man who futilely objected twice daily to his fireman's habit of bringing his dog along on the run, had had little to do but stare at the distant blue San Juans on one side and the violet peaks of the Sangre de Cristos on the other as the train sailed down the wide San Luis Valley into Alamosa, but there had been both livestock and game on the tracks from there on, and light snow on Cumbres Pass. Naturally. The San Juan extension of the Denver & Rio Grande was a slow and snaky route, inching along the Toltec Gorge, twisting over the Continental Divide and back and forth across the Colorado-New Mexico line, and since it was troublesome at best, new trouble had to be watched for carefully. As the engineer always said, if you've ever hit a bull elk on a four per cent grade at a speed of forty miles an hour, you know what it can do to engine and tender, so he'd wriggled with frustration from Alamosa on. The fireman's dog, made nervous by the engineer's impatience, all but jumped out of the cab in a spasm of barking on this final leg of the curve into Durango, but it was only a dog on the track and some mules beside it. The engineer ignored both the brakes and his fireman's reproachful look and reached for the dangling cord of the train whistle, barreling onward. He was neither pleased nor displeased that the dog leaped off the tracks in plenty of time. Hit a dog, and you only get a little bump. But hit a bull elk on a downslope at forty miles an hour, well, as he always said . . .

116

Calvin Fairchild, inside the third car, said to his uncle, "Durango! Won't be more'n five or ten minutes now." They both peered happily through the filthy train window, trying to see ahead, and they had no attention to spare for the four running figures that whipped past on the other side of the train.

"I never seen the beat of such country," Calvin's uncle said. "Tell you what, Calvin. If the animals are feeling up to it, let's buy us a couple of saddles and take them home cross-country instead of shipping them home in a boxcar. We couldn't see out of a boxcar, lest we cracked the door open and froze. A-course, it all depends on what shape the animals is in."

"Not altogether, Uncle Raleigh," Calvin said. He gestured to the invisible mass of the San Juans, now to the northeast of them. "Shortest way riding would be across Wolf Creek. I took the wagon over it once last summer, but never again. It's one humdinger of a pass. And it'll be getting itself snowed in just about any time now. Old Wolf Creek, it's near eleven thousand feet high, and they say it gets more snow than any pass in Colorado. Up to eight hundred inches of snow a winter."

"Lordy, Lordy," said Uncle Raleigh. "Forget I mentioned it. Train's slowing down, isn't it, Calvin? Is my hat on straight? Do I look all right? I don't want to go disgracing you in front of your young lady friend."

"Aw, Miss Hicks isn't my lady friend," said Calvin. "She's just a friend." But Calvin straightened his own hat and dusted the tips of his boots and was the first man on his feet when the conductor came through, crying, "Durango, Durango, all out for Durango."

Twelve

THE MEETING at the Durango depot was every bit as bad as Agatha Hicks feared it would be, and then things got worse. Hope reborn and as quickly deferred was cruel, and frustration made them all frantic. They lost a full day at Angus M'Taggart's insistence. Once he was able to comprehend what he'd done, he seemed positive somehow that the animals would have gone back west to his cabin. Agatha grabbed at the chance that he might be right. She sent Jack the stableman to rent a heavy mountain wagon, and when it became obvious that they would be benighted en route and she therefore couldn't go with them, she retired into silence and stayed awake most of the night wishing she'd been born a boy. But they came back empty-handed the next morning, Jack all sour and complaining he'd caught a cold. It took Superintendent Hicks' clerk and the office boy both running all over town before Agatha's efforts turned up the first report—the vicious mad dog that had tried to bite Mrs. Bert Townsend's two moppets on Monday had attacked them again Tuesday afternoon at a rancher's stock tank. Well, if it didn't actually attack them, it had run at them, without provocation, while her two darlings were innocently attempting to catch a tribe of ducks on hominy-baited fishhooks. Well, the dog *did* start to follow those vicious mules to the tank to drink, and it *would* have attacked the boys if they hadn't thrown rocks at it, and there was no denying it.

Calvin, his Uncle Raleigh, and M'Taggart all rushed out to the stock tank, and while they were gone a second report narrowed the direction. It came from two Cornish miners, friends of Jack's, who had tried to catch three stray mules, two red, one black, but a red mule kicked, and "the bugger 'urted Colin, 'e did. 'E bust the bloody wing of 'im." The mine they worked was eighteen miles from town near Los Piños River, on the way to Wolf Creek Pass.

Agatha sent Jack to find Calvin and his companions. Before they got back she thought she had confirmation of the animals' route, courtesy of her father, Superintendent Hicks, from an ore wagon unloading at the smelter. "Three mules and a dog seen by sluice on Squaw Creek last evening," Superintendent Hicks noted in a hasty scrawl. "I want baked ham for dinner, and tell Patsy applesauce. I can't stand those pickled crabapples."

When Calvin and the others returned, they held a council of war in the breakfast room, since all three men looked so uncomfortable at the mere mention of a parlor. "Squaw Creek," explained Agatha, "that's thirty miles toward Wolf Creek Pass. That puts them near halfway, and traveling fast."

"We'd better get going then," Calvin said.

"All right, Jack," Agatha said to the stableman. "You hurry straight back to Whitney's and rent that mountain wagon again, but tell Mr. Whitney I want fresh horses. Mr. Hillman, I expect you'll be going up with Mr. Fairchild, won't you?"

M'Taggart mumbled, "Me too, but it'd better be saddle horses, not a wagon. Wagon couldn't get through the pass."

With sobriety, M'Taggart had recovered his reticence, and if Agatha hadn't been so fretted she would have been amused at the mutual awkwardness of the shy harelip and the retiring Scot. She argued, "But there's no snow on the pass now. The Durango *Record* said it melted off just about as quick as it fell."

"There's more snow coming," M'Taggart said reluctantly. "Lots of it. Can't you feel it on the wind?"

"Indeed I can't, Mr. M'Taggart," Agatha said. "You just couldn't ask for a prettier day."

120

"All right, well, but I noticed out by the tank—all the birds, they're coming down."

Yellow sunshine fell warmly on Agatha's back, but she shivered. There was a puzzled expression on the uncle's face, and she explained. "The migrating flocks just seem to stop and wait if there's a storm on its way. They know somehow when it's not safe to try to cross the high mountains. They flutter down like leaves. If Mr. M'Taggart says they're coming down, likely there'll be a bird tucked up under every rose bush in the garden."

M'Taggart nodded. "Wild creatures can always tell."

Calvin's uncle didn't care for that. "Well, then, so could Calvin's Jebs," he said. "Mules are smart. They're twice as smart as horses. That's why it takes twice as long to train them. If it snows, they'll just hole up somewhere until it stops. Now, I admit I don't know much about snow and nothing about mountains, but if I can't track three mules and a dawg in a direction we're dead certain they're going, my name isn't Raleigh Hillman. Calvin, we'd best hie ourselves to some mercantile store and see to bedrolls and the like."

"I can tend to all that here," Agatha said. She rose, but a mumble from Calvin stopped her.

"I sure do appreciate everything you've done, but there's no need to put yourself out anymore," he said. "You too, Mr. M'Taggart. Uncle Raleigh and me, we'll be back before you know it with the animals. Uncle Raleigh's one fine tracker. I reckon he's just about the finest hunter in all of Claiborne Parish. And if the animals get over the pass before us, we'll just track them on up the San Luis Valley and right home to Salida. Won't we, Uncle Raleigh?"

"You bet," Uncle Raleigh said, but M'Taggart shook his head.

"We get heavy enough weather, there's nothing that's going to go up over that pass except maybe wolves," he said. "Snow can really layer down on Wolf Creek. Flakes as big as your hand. Me, I'm betting the mules hold back, and we'll find

121

them waiting like the birds on this side of the Divide. I'm going with you, of course. It's the least I can do, and I'm pretty useful in the mountains. Miss 'Icks, you tell them."

Called upon as an ally, Agatha did tell them, and she sent Jack on the run to the livery stable and her two servant girls scurrying for blankets and tarps and provisions. Poppa and his baked ham could wait. Agatha didn't forget a big bag of mixed oats and corn for the mules and a supply of jerky for the dog, and she only lamented that she had no venison for the poor fellow when M'Taggart confided that the old dog liked it.

"Did Mr. Fairchild's dog eat good for you?" she whispered to M'Taggart. "I couldn't get him to eat too good for me." They were outside now, and Calvin and his uncle were arranging the bags and blankets on three bored-looking saddle horses. They could feel the full force of a wind that indeed suddenly seemed chillier. Agatha pulled her shawl tighter around her shoulders.

"He ate good enough, but I couldn't get him to sit still for helping him much with his sore paws," M'Taggart whispered back. "Tying him, now, maybe it put him off his feed a bit, but it sure was a good idea for those sore paws."

They looked at each other, then simultaneously looked guiltily at Calvin. Agatha hadn't had the heart to tell him how used up his poor old dog had seemed.

Calvin apparently saw them look his way, and he came to them. "You talking about Nemo?" he said. His voice was cheerful, but his eyes had regained their distracted, apprehensive look. "I've been meaning to apologize for him. I'm afraid he might not have acted very friendly. He never was much for tail-wagging, all the time I've had him. But I just know he appreciated everything y'all did for him."

"Now, listen, he acted just fine, like the gentleman he is," M'Taggart said, and Agatha saw that the Scot had no more intention than she of worrying Calvin with the animal's wild and distrustful manner. "He just had big business on his mind—looking after those mules."

122

Calvin nodded. "It tickles me like anything, to think all this time they've been making a beeline for home. Well, I guess if we're going to catch up with them, we'd better get going. Uncle Raleigh says everything looks shipshape to him."

They left at a fast trot. Agatha stood waving in the sunshine. The sky was a clear, clean blue, with none of the gathering gray haze that in ripe summer might mean rain but at autumn's swift coming in the big mountains meant one thing, snow. But the wind seemed more cutting by the minute. Agatha went into the house, trying not to mind that no one, especially Calvin, had apparently even thought of suggesting that she, a mere woman, should accompany them.

She tried to estimate how long they would be gone. They'd face, say, sixty miles. Eighty, if the animals managed to reach Wolf Creek's summit. The rescuers couldn't possibly start up the pass before tomorrow, and more probably the day after and then the return journey would take at least two more days. It seemed a long time to have to sit and wonder.

Agatha restlessly made a circuit of her father's house, looking for something to do, but she'd trained the Cornish serving girls well, and nothing bid for her attention except ordering his dinner. She went to her room. It was already occupied by four cats. A fat gray cat with a skinny tail lay luxuriously between her bed pillows. A calico cat was curled in a tight ball, paws tucked in, on the foot of her bed. A black lay sprawled in a beam of sunshine on the carpet, and her latest rescue case, the little cripple named Scraps, huddled by the empty hearth as if hoping someone would kindle a fire.

Two cats curled up, two lying comfortably. M'Taggart and the birds might be right about a snowstorm threatening, but unless the cats lied, which they never did, there was only a fifty-fifty chance that it would strike today.

Thirteen

NOT EVEN MIGRATORY BIRDS could predict weather with complete precision, and the storm took its time in coming. Clear skies lingered the next morning. A chattering flock of green-tailed towhees en route to winter grounds in Texas decided to leave their shelter in a thicket of scrub oak and wing over the Continental Divide. An off-route great crested flycatcher on its way from southern Canada to eastern Mexico followed suit. The other birds stayed put, but a feeling of urgency drove the four-footed travelers on. By late morning, the dog and the mules had pushed into the valley that cradled the San Juan River, and the peaks of the Divide jutted boldly before them.

The river, fed by each winter's storms on the San Juan peaks, ran west to join the Colorado River. The same snows melted through a narrow, glacier-carved canyon on the east side of the peaks to become the south fork of the Rio Grande. A wagon road had been blasted from the mountains alongside the two watercourses, switchbacking over Wolf Creek Pass. The mountains squeezed too tightly to allow the animals to travel parallel with the road, and the dog might actually have traveled on it had not their passage through and beyond Durango been marked by so much rock throwing and attempts at capture. But now the dog feared roads more than ever. They smelled of the enemy, people, and he refused to set foot on this one. The valley began to narrow, and he harried the mules away from it.

When they finally turned upward, they did so in a small

canyon, but it deadended in a broken granite wall, at the foot of which brooded a deep, still pool. Old Jeb, confident of his sure-footedness, tried to pick a way up through the moss-covered rocks. A hindfoot slipped against a head-sized boulder that bounced once, twice, and into dark water. Old Jeb turned to watch. The boulder sank with apparent leisureliness, gleaming whitely, then turned green as the waters slowly covered it, then was lost in blackness. Old Jeb turned in a space scarcely large enough for his four hoofs and climbed down. They would try elsewhere.

Because the animals climbed at random, they climbed in earnest for the first time. It was easy enough to avoid steep rock faces, but between them and the eastern foot of the mountains lay some forty-five miles of sprawling slopes and peaks reaching to heights of thirteen- and fourteen-thousand feet. There was no avoiding a steep, steady incline, and the pace quickly began to tell on the old dog. The food and care received from the hands first of M'Taggart, then Agatha, had gotten him this far, but behind those interludes of rest and good rations lay the long shadow of hunger and deep fatigue. The days, the weeks, the months—the dog couldn't count the time that had passed. He could only endure each hour as it came.

And now, the higher they climbed, the harder his heaving sides had to fight for breath. His eyes and nose began to run. Worse, the animals couldn't avoid rock underfoot, and the newly healing pads of his paws wore quickly back to tender flesh. They made a slow advance, frustrated all too often by gigantic slide areas where gravity and the snows of past winters had sent rock crashing into timber to form an impenetrable jumble. Then the animals would climb down again, two hundred feet, five hundred feet, and feverishly seek a way around the slide.

The first snow flurry hit them in late afternoon as Old Jeb signaled it was time to rest at the foot of a naked scar left by yet another slide. But, teasingly, as if only to hint at its power, the snowfall lasted only a few minutes. A great silence settled over the mountains. The dog became aware of the wheeze of labored breathing, both his own and the mules, but soon their gasping eased and there was no sound at all. There was no wind. Not a pine needle whispered. Then came a faint, far-off howling, guttural yet musical, and all the animals swung their heads and listened apprehensively in the direction they had come.

There was nothing below them but a sea of dark, silent timber. The howling faded, and the silence settled again, profound and queerly ominous, and no matter how hard the old dog listened he could hear nothing but the hard, irregular thudding of his own heart.

The dog lay down in the thin snow, the better to rest. But still he listened, trying to fathom with his ears what no eyes could see—not just the approach of a hunter, a wolf, but the triggering of a killer storm. The peculiar hush of the mountains told him it couldn't be much longer.

Old Jeb, usually so calm, was becoming increasingly nervous, and he moved long before the dog was ready. The dog waited to be sure that Young Jeb and Margaret were going to follow voluntarily. He was glad of the additional few seconds' breather, but, snorting, stomachs rumbling with their motion, the two younger mules rolled out to catch up with Old Jeb, who was already angling upward again, climbing toward another stand of tall pines. The dog reluctantly moved too.

White pain burned with the first step. He whimpered and would have sat down, but the mules were getting too far ahead of him. He risked another step, then another, and then the pain became the familiar companion he had known since they'd started up the mountain. The light snow should have been soothing, but it wasn't. It burned like the pain. He climbed stiffly onward. There wasn't much time, and there was nowhere else to go.

That night, when the real snow staged a dress rehearsal, the dog and the mules were still far below the Divide, bedded down in an aspen grove. The first flakes were large and powdery and floated dreamily from a starless sky that lacked the faintest breath of wind. They melted as they hit the ground. Eventually the snowflakes hit without melting. As the animals slept on, the snowfall thickened, then really dumped. It fell at the rate of a foot an hour for nearly two hours. At the top of the pass, strong winds began to toy with the new snow, piling it in drifts, but at the animals' altitude it lay in an even mantle, and dawn brought bright sun to lavish diamonds upon its white glory. Less than glorious to the animals, the snow was a thick white sea through which they floundered, but they continued to labor upward. The worst of the storm had not yet come.

Camped nearly fifty flat miles from Durango near an eroded rock formation inevitably named Chimney Rock, the animals' frustrated rescuers got no snow at all. They learned of it ten miles farther on at a lumber mill near the last flatland settlement, where they stopped to ask whether anyone had seen a dog and three lost mules. No one had, but the millhands allowed it was chancy weather to be trying for the Divide.

"I almost wish we had gotten snow," Calvin said when they rode out. "Three mules on melting snow wouldn't tiptoe like fairies, would they? They'd tear up the ground plenty." So far, they had found no tracks, and Calvin was worried they were on the wrong route.

M'Taggart worried too, but for a different reason. Up high, there'd be melt on top of the snow. Then it would ice over, which would make the going even harder. M'Taggart caught a troubled look on the face of the uncle from Louisiana and knew him for a good countryman who could read even unfamiliar weather.

They rode four more miles by the time they caught their first clear view of the snow-covered peaks, and by that time they were into thin snow themselves. Then, in the snow, Calvin finally spotted a clear set of tracks a mile beyond the foot of the pass, and he wouldn't listen either to M'Taggart or his uncle when they told him the tracks were horse. Nothing would do but to follow them. They led to the cabin of a prospector M'Taggart had sometimes seen around Durango, an old-timer who never got the heebie-jeebies about a little early snow but who planned to sit this storm out snug at home. He had seen no dogs or mules.

One hour more, three hours left of daylight, and they heard the mournful music of wolves calling a pack together. The sound didn't bother M'Taggart, but the looks of the sky did. Lead gray was overtaking blue, and they were still at least ten hard, zigzagging miles from the summit. The temperature was dropping rapidly.

Yet another hour of labored climbing, two hours left of daylight, and they encountered the first layer of ice freezing rapidly to form a crust atop the ever-deepening snow. They stopped to rest the horses. The snow layer was unbroken. No traffic through here. But as they rested, two men in a one-horse buggy came around a sharp bend in the road. M'Taggart and the uncle involuntarily exchanged a glance full of dread. Ice clung heavily in the spokes of the buggy wheels and even frosted the horse's mane.

The men hailed them without wasting time with greetings. "How much farther out of the pass?" one called. He sounded hostile, angry even, but it was at the weather, not at them.

"About two hours' ride," M'Taggart answered. The two men looked like drummers. Bowler hats. Black suits. Both wore fur-lined overcoats, but he saw that they were shivering uncontrollably. He added, "Don't guess you've seen a black-and-white dog and three mules up the pass, have you?"

"We didn't see anything but snow," the other man replied shortly. "Is there any place we can take shelter around here? A hotel?"

"Miners' shacks. Not much else. It's pretty clear from here

down. If your horse can make it, you'd better go on in to Pagosa Springs."

"Dag Burnit, my feet are frozen!" the first man growled. "Where're these miners' shacks?"

"Look to your right just before you get to the river. You'll see smoke. That's Jake Flynt. He'll take you in, I guess."

"The river? But that must be miles! We've got to get out of this cold."

M'Taggart knew they'd break into the first cabin they came to. There was a cluster of cabins by a new mining operation three or four miles back, no one staying there, but M'Taggart said nothing and watched the drummers flog their weary horse into a staggering walk. Maybe they'd pass the mining operation before dark and see it, maybe they wouldn't. It wasn't all that cold yet. If they'd get out of that wagon and walk some warmth into their feet instead of leaving all the work to their one tired horse, they could make their way across the snow line easy.

The uncle called after the slowly moving buggy, "What's it like up ahead?"

"You wouldn't believe it," the second man called back.

"Plenty of snow?"

"Enough. We stopped overnight last night to wait it out on the east side of the summit. But from there on it was slush and ice."

Now the wolf call came again, rising and falling, and the drummers flogged their horse harder and jolted onward, while the uncle shot another glance at M'Taggart.

"No problem," M'Taggart said, meaning wolves. "They're miles away. Nothing carries like a wolf's wail. They're not interested in us anyway."

Calvin began to sputter, "My mules . . . ?"

"They're not interested in mules either," M'Taggart assured him. "A calf, a deer that's too slow—wolves aren't half what they're cracked up to be. They're only interested in an easy dinner. Eat field mice, most of the time. Must be tasty little things."

Calvin's eyes swung to a massive granite cliff that rose above them. Its top was lost in lead-gray snowclouds, behind which the real peaks hid their heads, aspiring skyward but tumbling down, down, down into a hundred gorges and a thousand valleys through which the hungry flatlands reached up and tried, with wind and frost and the sucking power of gravity, to drag the mountains down. "Dear God," Calvin said softly, "how'll we ever be able to find them in all of this?"

"Here, now," said the uncle, "what's a mountain but a patch of flatland that's got big ideas about itself? I say we make camp here for the night, and we'll see how things look tomorrow. How about it, Mr. M'Taggart? Reckon I ought to start getting up a big batch of firewood? It's going to be a cold night."

M'Taggart thought of the timber line and beyond, where rotted snow lay always on the north side of the larger rock outcroppings. It would be colder by far up there. Calvin must have spent time above timber line too, among the rock and lichen and the snow that stayed packed from early fall to late spring, for his hazel eyes looked as leaden as the sky. M'Taggart thought for a half hour, while he masterminded the arrangements for a cold night's rest, before he decided on the most heartening words of consolation: "If those two fool drummers could get over Wolf Creek before the big snow, anybody could get over it, including your animals." But he couldn't help thinking of the fate of livestock that got stranded in the mountains in a storm. Oh, they'd start moving down toward the valleys when they felt a storm coming, move long before the deer and elk, but if they got caught, they often stood and waited until their nostrils filled with snow—just waited where they were until they suffocated.

In the end, not wanting to get anybody's hopes up only to have them dashed down again, M'Taggart said nothing at all.

131

Fourteen

BEFORE DAWN, the storm made its final assault on the peaks. The snowflakes seemed beautiful and innocent in the beginning. A few powdery flakes whispered through the darkness, touching the exhausted animals so lightly that none awoke. The flakes swirled and thickened and began to freeze around the animals' mouths and nostrils, but still they slept on. Their second day on the mountain had been a day of cruel exertion, and their night's rest had been broken by the sound of tree limbs groaning and sometimes snapping under a coat of ice. The dog would break a frigid bed for himself through the icy crust of the snow and settle down, then the groaning of the trees would disturb him, and he would flounder out and drive the mules a few yards farther and try to sleep again. They were still on the west side of the summit, above the line where aspens could grow and into the last of the pines just below timber line, and the dog finally blundered into a dense growth of dwarf juniper that acted as a good windbreak. He succumbed to heavy slumber, while the mules huddled together under the pines and turned their tails to the wind.

They wouldn't have been separated, even with the coming of the storm, had it not been for Young Jeb. He slept the least of any. He took exception to Margaret's being in the middle of the huddle, and, awakening over and over, he was the first to become aware of the rapid build-up of the new snow, which announced itself by falling with a thump from an overweighted branch. Then Young Jeb caught a whiff of something wild and worrisome on the wind and began to stamp

133

nervously. The other mules roused briefly but dropped off to sleep again. Another thump and Young Jeb nervously took a few blind steps into the sprawl of junipers, and a Thing clawed at his hock. It was a trailing branch, but Young Jeb didn't wait to investigate. He took to his heels, plunging blindly into the dark curtain of the snow.

The dog awoke instantly, for in that instant he too caught a strange scent that cried, "Danger!" The morning was far too cold for scent to spread freely, and as quickly as the dog caught it, it was gone. He didn't know where the danger came from. He did know that one of his charges was gone, and he floundered off in pursuit. Old Jeb and Margaret floundered after him.

In the darkness, in the cold, in their confusion, the animals quickly lost one another. Wind and a sudden timidity caught at the dog. An ice-encrusted beard of gray lichen flapped stiffly on a tree ahead, and he veered away from it. He hit a slope of solid ice underlying the powdery new snow and slid a few feet sideways. He continued in his random direction. Timber line was only three or four hundred feet above him now, and beyond it the wind and snow ruled.

By staying at the edge of the now sparse and wind-twisted timber, the dog fought his way around the crest of the mountain, not over it. He crossed the great line that divided rivers between the eastward and westward oceans without knowing he had crossed it. He halted only when the wind, now whipping at his back, brought him a suggestion of mule.

He barked repeatedly. His voice was blown away by the wind, but Young Jeb was already plunging and sliding in his direction. Downwind, five adult wolves padding homeward atop the icy crust of the old snow stopped and listened to the sound.

The wolves' stomachs were distended by some twenty pounds of venison each, fruit of a long night's patient hunting. Each had curled up to nap in the snow after feasting, but after they had awakened and nosed the leftovers of their kill, which

134

comprised little but the neck and head, they had routinely headed home for a more satisfying sleep, each wolf stepping precisely in the footsteps of the leader, for whom the dubious pleasure of breaking through the new snow building up on the crust was the privilege of leadership.

But this was the wolves' range. No other canid had a right here, and they turned uphill to investigate and defend, and, not incidentally, to satisfy a curiosity that rivaled a cat's. They crept, gray shadows in the first glimmers of a gray dawn.

Young Jeb spotted them first and squealed his terror. The wolves' savagery was directed at the old dog and they felt only a curious interest in the mule, but, mulelike, he didn't suspect this. The dog jerked around, alerted by Young Jeb's squealing, and his backbone and tail both instantly wilted.

Less well fed, the wolves might have concentrated on the mule. And confronting another wolf, they might have allowed him to indicate submission and, after a growling lesson about violating another pack's range, let him cringe away, nipping at his rear to give him speed. But there was no question of the dog's merely surrendering.

A heavy-shouldered female wolf, quicker witted than the others, identified the dog first. He *was* a dog, and he was old, and fatigue made his movements feeble. The female's hackles stiffened, and she bared her teeth in a snarl that showed red gums. The five wolves circled out to ring the intruders, their queer, light eyes fixed on the dog with the unreasoning revulsion that wild animals feel for the old. Come to investigate, they stayed to kill.

The first deep growl that whipped away on the wind came from the aggressive female. The pack milled, the female moving to the dog's right with another wolf following her, and two other wolves to the left, leaving one of their platoon growling in the middle. Young Jeb squealed again and reared, kicking out with his forefeet. The dog ducked and scrambled a few feet to the side. But solely because the mule was there to be defended, he stood his ground to defend himself. The muscles

135

of the dog's forehead and nose stood out like cords as his face furrowed in threat. Growling, he hunched his body and lowered his head until it almost touched ground. He swung it back and forth, trying to watch all five wolves at once in the fast-falling snow.

A big male on his left attempted a rush. Terror and anger lurched in the dog's stomach. The dog didn't think. He was guided by something quicker than his mind—an impetus that lived in the nerves and muscle. He reared to meet the attack, forepaws grasping for purchase on the wolf's shoulder and teeth grinding sickeningly on teeth as they closed in a deadly embrace. They lost balance and rolled on the snow. The old dog fought to get under the wolf, where raking hind claws could reach the wolf's stomach and jaws lock on the exposed jugular, but just as suddenly the male wolf was snapping at his genitals and another gray form, the aggressive female, was at his head, gaping jaws trying for a suffocating death hold over his muzzle. By a violent twist, he jerked away. The female slashed his cheek with razorlike teeth and leaped clear. The old dog's battle tactic of slash, then jump back, was of little value here. In the wolves, he had met the masters of the art.

Harried from the rear by the male wolf, attacked boldly from the front by the female, the dog backed even closer to Young Jeb's plunging form, for even as he snapped desperately but futilely at his attackers, he saw the other wolves closing in. They were aroused. They would take the mule as well as the dog. The old dog was terrified.

But a fourteen-hundred-pound mule is not a deer or even an eight-hundred-pound elk. Young Jeb may first have squealed in fright, but now he brayed a battle call. He joined the fight, kicking with cannonball hoofs like the mare that mothered him, circling and biting like the jackass that was his father.

And suddenly Young Jeb and the dog were not fighting alone. Fourteen hundred more pounds of frenzied red mule kicked the heavy-shouldered female wolf before she could disengage her fangs from the old dog's shoulder. Profiled against

136

the snow-blurred skyline, a black mule, slower but no less maddened by the danger to her herd, came charging after Old Jeb.

The big male wolf flung himself upon his side, but Old Jeb's huge yellow teeth clamped over the top of his head. The wolf thrashed madly, throwing his heavy body from side to side, fighting to escape from the blunt but granitelike teeth, and when he fought free the hoofs caught him, one, two, to chest and side. Bones cracked, then the hoofs caught him again, catapulting him down the slope. The wolf lay still, not dead but stunned, bleeding from the mouth, and there four plunging black hoofs overtook him and crushed out his life.

The aggressive female wolf got away, limping after two of the other wolves who fled before her, but a second wolf died in the blood-covered snow. The mules continued to trample and plunge long after the two wolves were dead, then sniffed and snorted at the two shapeless masses of brown fur and entrails and blood, until another figure fearfully and cautiously tried to rise.

The old dog had to try and try again before he could get his legs under him. Like the two dead wolves, he oozed blood. The torn cheek bled the most. He was bewildered and panicky over the smell of his own blood dripping on the snow, and for a long time he stood with drooping head, swaying, fearful that the maddened mules might attack him as quickly as they had the wolves. Whirling snowflakes melted on his back. His body began to stiffen. He forced himself to motion only when he saw that the mules were leaving.

Young Jeb still stamped around the two motionless forms in the snow, but Old Jeb started purposefully downhill, with Margaret close behind. The dog took a step, but the foreleg that had hurt him so long after the fight with the Indian dogs doubled up under him. He fell.

Downslope a dozen yards, Young Jeb uttered a nervous, hiccuping bray, and the old dog whimpered and wagged his bobbed tail, a quick, frightened wag, telling the mule, "Don't worry. I'm coming." He rose and stumbled toward Young Jeb, one more step, only to fall again in the snow. He thrust his head out, shaking it. He was terror-stricken to see that Young Jeb was turning to follow the other mules.

The old dog thrashed, as if trying to swim through the snow, and sank in deeper, but he regained the surface and crawled, inching his way over the thin crust of ice, making a last effort not to be left behind in the awful immensity on the top of the world. With rheum running from his eyes he saw Young Jeb disappear into the silently falling snow. Every cell in his brain and every nerve in his body said, "Follow!" But his muscles would not obey. He moaned low in his throat and tried again, and this time he fell through the crust of yesterday's ice and lay still.

Already five hundred feet below the summit, Old Jeb suddenly hesitated, and Margaret, following close behind, rammed into him. He showed her his teeth and nervously lashed his tail. Before him lay a white, narrow path broken through the snow, and the path demanded examination. First he smelled it carefully, thinking wolves, but there was no scent. Gingerly, he stepped upon it, and his hoofs became aware of something beneath them. A hardness. A smoothness. He looked around for Young Jeb and the dog, but the snowfall was still thick and he couldn't see them.

No matter. His whole consciousness shouted at him that he must get far down out of these mountains and away from this storm. And beneath him lay a path hammered out of stone and earth by succeeding generations of bighorn sheep. The path was narrow, and it had a hundred curls and wiggles and detours, but it was a path over the range. A herd of elk, waiting as was their habit until a storm actually materialized, had already taken it to seek refuge in the valleys. Snowflakes hurried down to cover their footsteps.

Old Jeb wasted no time taking the path. He was tired and frightened, and somewhere to the east of these mountains was a wide valley he had begun to remember clearly. You trotted north up the valley, and then there was an easy climb up a little pass, and then to the left as you trotted down the pass there was the side road that led to a mountain cabin with a stinking photographer's wagon on one side of it, and on the other side a big, fenced mule lot with a snug barn in which shelled corn and oats were doled out generously. Old Jeb had a vivid memory of lazing in that barn eating the corn, and he was cold and wet snow had balled up in his hoofs all day long, and he was ready for a long, warm rest in that barn.

But a second thought occurred to him, and he stopped again so abruptly that Margaret once more ran into him. Young Jeb was supposed to be in the barn beside him, and the other creature, the dog, was supposed to wander into the barn from time to time, and lie in the sun outside it, and disappear into the cabin and reappear, barking, if any human came up the road by the stream in front of the cabin. Young Jeb and the dog were part of Old Jeb's home.

Hmmp, there was Young Jeb behind Margaret. Old Jeb hadn't noticed his arrival, and he was very pleased to see the younger mule. Now the dog would come. Old Jeb stamped a minute or two, waiting for the dog to come and take charge.

But the dog didn't come. Old Jeb was eager to get to the barn and the corn. He got tired of waiting and started down the path again, willing the others to follow.

But it gave him an uneasy feeling, for him to have to be the leader instead of the dog.

Only five miles below the summit on the west side, another trio looked up through the veil of falling snow at an unbroken wall of snowy, tree-clad mountainside, and Calvin's uncle wondered, not for the first time, how a road could possibly be hidden in those heights. But, for that matter, he couldn't see the roadbed his benumbed feet were standing on, and he had only M'Taggart's word for it that one was there. In the hour that they had waited to see what the snow would do since they

139

broke camp at dawn, their campsite had filled in with new, smooth snow, and the only clear footprints Uncle Raleigh could see were those under his own boots.

"Well, Calvin?" he finally said. He reluctantly turned a pinched, cold-reddened face to hear Calvin's decision, and he wasn't surprised when Calvin couldn't seem to put it into direct words.

"Well, I say we lead the horses," Calvin said quietly. He only gestured to indicate the direction—downward. "We'd be too much weight, the way this snow is lying. Wouldn't we, Mr. M'Taggart?"

"That's about the size of it," M'Taggart said. "We'll take turns breaking trail. Kind of slide along easy, and we won't keep going through the crust."

"I'll do the trail breaking," Calvin said. He suited his action to his words and turned downhill, snowplowing with his boots. His horse followed skittishly.

To get so near, Uncle Raleigh thought. But the last five miles up were an impossibility. As for getting down . . . He waited a moment for M'Taggart to collect his horse and asked, "We going to have much trouble getting out?"

"I don't think so," M'Taggart said. "Seems to me the snow is thinning, and then there'll be less of it anyway as we go down. But we'll want to move right along. When it stops snowing, it'll start getting really cold right quick."

"How cold?"

"Well, ten, twenty below. I still say we'd better take turns breaking trail. It's too much work for Calvin to do all by himself."

"No, leave him be, at least for a while," Uncle Raleigh said. "He needs something to do. It'll take his mind off things. I guess there's no hope at all for his animals, is there?"

M'Taggart shook his head. "I could have told him when we woke up to all this snow this morning, but I just didn't have the heart. The mules, well, if they'd been in better shape they

140

might have stood at least a chance. But there's not a hope in the world that that poor old dog could have made it."

"Poor things," said Uncle Raleigh. "Poor Calvin. It's like they died twice."

They fell into line, both silent, and followed Calvin on the long trip down from the mountains.

Fifteen

THE FARTHER Old Jeb traveled down the sheep trail, the more out of sorts he became. The dog's truancy just didn't seem sensible to the big mule. Old Jeb was normally a patient sort, long accustomed to the dog's habit of sneaking off on mysterious errands, but this was ridiculous. Snow was still falling. New dangers could be approaching. The corn and the barn were waiting. Old Jeb paused and snorted the special snort that carried over long distances, calling to a missing member of the herd. The dog still didn't come, and he bared his teeth temperishly. What was that creature doing this time? Where was the dog?

Old Jeb understood the dog no better than the dog understood him. While he granted the dog the same tolerance and grave comradeship that he granted the other members of what he regarded as his herd, he certainly didn't love the dog as an individual. As well love a fish or a bird in the sky or that other unfathomable creature, the man. But the herd was supposed to stay together. The dog was supposed to be somewhere near his heels. In pursuit of the old, boring sameness that he preferred in his life, Old Jeb turned and retraced his footsteps, most reluctantly, leading the other mules in the wrong direction, uphill.

When the old dog returned to consciousness, nearly a half hour later, all three mules were standing in a ring around him. They couldn't tend his wounds, and wouldn't have thought of it if they could, and they couldn't help him stumble from the wintry walls of the mountains, and wouldn't have thought to do that either, but they could wait for the barn and the corn and the dog that was supposed to be with them. And wait they did.

Old Jeb was gratified to see the first stirring of the shaggy creature, still smelling scarily of blood. He stretched his neck and nibbled the dog's withers, in mule greeting and inquiry. The dog whined, but he didn't get up, and Old Jeb cast his big eyes down at the recumbent form and all but sighed. This was no time for the dog to be troublesome. He nibbled at the dog again and stood back to await the effect.

There, the creature was on his feet, although not all of them. They could leave. But how slow the dog was. He had that mysterious limp again, his bad leg doubling under him every few steps. Ugh, was that fresh blood, or was it the nasty smell from the trampled, bloodstained battleground? Here was the path his own heavy body had broken down to the sheep trail. Now they could hurry. If the dog only would. One might as well paw down through this snow and seek out a mouthful or two of frozen grass. The dog was coming so slowly, one would have to wait again.

For a time, snowflakes drifted down on the path to melt on the blood still slowly dripping from the cheek of the limping dog. But gradually the fall of the snow stopped, and so did the bleeding, and the path constructed by the sheep and snow-plowed by the dog's mules led him away from the mountains.

Snow in the mountains, frost in the broad, mountain-bordered valley to which the animals finally came. When frost hit, the green chlorophyl in the leaves withdrew into branches and trunks, and the real color of the leaves appeared, yellow like the sun. After frost came Indian summer, and the leaves of the aspens on the mountains' flanks turned saffron and orange and flaming red, changing shades by the day, but the cottonwoods in the valley only turned yellow. Later, like the aspen leaves, they would brown and drop, but as the animals inched up the

144

valley the leaves were bright yellow and fluttered crisply, and the mules had to nudge only a few aside on the ground as they hungrily cropped grass that was only a little dry and wonderfully nourishing.

For the last seventy miles, the dog tried to survive on grubs and crickets and a few vinegary ants—whatever he could find in the places Old Jeb halted to graze. Sometimes the dog chewed bark. Once he filled his stomach with hay, cut but not yet baled at an outlying farm the mules stopped to raid, but the dog only vomited the hay out again. Even more than food, he craved water, and he drank it in choking gulps whenever they chanced upon a creek or irrigation ditch, but Old Jeb, able to travel comfortably with only the occasional drink, detoured to search for water far too rarely for the dog. Accommodating himself to the dog's painfully slow pace was the limit of Old Jeb's ability to bethink himself of the other animal's incomprehensible frailty.

For the dog, every mile was a stupendous accomplishment. Although he didn't recover the use of his crippled leg, he hurried as fast as he was able after the mules, not only because he feared they might leave him again but because in his blurred consciousness he still regarded them as his charges. And as the valley began to narrow perceptively into a V-shape and they reached the gentle pass at its narrowest end, the dog began to hurry even faster. Over this pass was a certain side road, and at the end of this road a certain cabin. If he could just get ahead of Old Jeb, he would be the first one there.

But the old dog was the last of the animals to lope across the log bridge spanning the clear, fast-running stream in front of Calvin Fairchild's cabin. No matter how swiftly he hobbled, the mules trotted faster. He lost sight of them at the log bridge, and within seconds forgot all about his charges. There was the wagon!

The dog sniffed the wagon over hastily, trying to make sure that he was not making another mistake, but he was distracted. Right beside the wagon was the cabin. And even through the closed doors and shuttered windows he could smell some marvelous aroma that centered in the place he had ached for so long—his kitchen.

Stale scent of sulfocyanide from the wagon. Fresh scent of sun-warmed pine resin beading on the logs of the cabin. Mouth-watering scent of meat—two kinds of meat—there inside the kitchen. Only the faintest, lingering scent of man. The old dog accepted the familiar scents of home with immense pleasure, but without surprise, and, just as Old Jeb had led the other mules directly to the barn, the dog limped straight past the wagon and to the kitchen door and scratched on it, hard. Then he waited.

It was disconcerting that the man didn't come immediately. Sometimes he kept the dog waiting, of course. This usually happened on nights when rare and wonderful scents of skunk or passing dogs or putrid fox carcass blew on the wind, and the dog ecstatically ranged the wild luxury of the mountains. Then when the dog returned to the cabin the man would be asleep, and the dog, ready for the warm corner beside the stove, would have to scratch interminably to wake the man, either that or let himself in. Getting in by himself was difficult, so the dog always preferred to wake the man.

But no matter how long he scratched now, the man didn't come. The dog was mystified. The wagon, the kitchen, the mules were all here, but the man was the one missing ingredient—not to mention a skilletful of jerked beef softened enough for old teeth to chew, or, if he was extraordinarily lucky, a helping of the meats he could smell so strongly inside the kitchen. Then the dog remembered that sometimes the man had ranged the mountains like himself, carrying the smelly, heavy object, his camera, and after a while he would return and go into the enclosed part of the wagon.

Something moved on the other side of the cabin. The dog pricked his ears, and his bobtail started to wag, and he limped hurriedly to meet the man, but it was only Old Jeb and Young

146

Jeb and Margaret, circling the cabin. The dog circled with them as they sniffed briskly and tried to look through the cabin's shuttered windows. The gate to the mule lot had been left open, but the barn was closed tight, and Old Jeb was more than ready for his corn and oats. Where was the man?

They soon realized that the man was absent. The doors weren't locked. No one locked houses in the area, and few houses even had locks, since thievery of household goods was largely unknown. Calvin Fairchild was a man who didn't even pull in his latch strings.

The latch string on the kitchen door caught the dog's attention. He studied it, trying to remember something about it, until Old Jeb gave up on the man and strolled into the hayfield where the dog had caught so many mice. The mule began to graze. Sparkling water ran always in the stream in front of the cabin. He could nap in the mule lot, drink from the stream, and dine in the field of wild hay. It would suffice.

Things were different for the dog. He scratched on the door again, from habit, not hope, and waited, inhaling deeply. With the smell of food came a reawakening of terrible need for it. A familiar scent wafting from the hayfield offered him an alternative—a meal of mouse. Of course.

The dog wobbled on his three good legs as he tracked the scent along a maze of inch-wide runways that the field mice had cut everywhere through the wild hay. When the scent became musky and strong, he poised himself. Head high. Eyes straining to catch the slightest movement in the grass. Aching forelegs straight, ready to stab downward if the first bite missed the mouse and it had to be flushed out of camouflaging immobility.

He couldn't believe it. Both the bite and the stab of the forepaws missed widely. He was rewarded only by a quick rustle. But there were other mice. He tracked and missed again, and tried again, always missing, until finally he forgot his years of mouse wisdom and began to dig, hurting, throwing dirt from

147

empty burrows the size of a teacup, from which the occupants had long since fled through their underground tunnels.

In one burrow, a quarter cup of grass seed had been thriftily stored. The dog gobbled the seed and instantly forgot that he had eaten anything at all and thought of the meat smell in the kitchen with increased longing. He turned back to the cabin.

It took considerable staring at the latch string, but then he remembered. To get in, he would have to grasp the latch string just so in his teeth and simultaneously rear against the door and jerk, and then the door would open, and the man would wake up and give him the meat. He was so tired that the simultaneous rear-up-and-jerk motion eluded him, and, as with the mice, he tried over and over before the door suddenly opened. He fell inside. The lame foreleg doubled under. He hardly noticed. He was in the kitchen at last. And there, hanging from the rafters over his head were the sources of the marvelous aroma—two country-cured hams and a glistening garland of homemade sausages.

The dog was polite about it. Even in an agony of hunger, he pushed into the main room of the cabin and sniffed every corner lengthily and completely, looking for the man. At the foot of the loft where the man slept, he stood staring upward, whining, but the scent already had told him the man wasn't there. He went back to the kitchen and looked up at the hams.

His nostrils flared. His mouth opened. A drop of saliva rolled from under his tongue and hung on his lower lip, and he licked several times, rapidly, and closed his mouth, but it promptly opened again. He yawned until the hinges of his jaws popped, staring at the two hams.

Finally he ducked his head and looked away guiltily. That was human food. On the long, long list of forbidden criminal activities, to touch human food unbidden was Forbidden Act Number One. But even if he wouldn't look, he couldn't help smelling, and helplessly his eyes went upward again to the hams.

148

He sat down, his one good foreleg supporting him, the lame one held a little off the floor, and he stared. More saliva beaded on his lower lip. He licked, but he wasn't quick enough this time and it fell to the wooden floor. Another drop fell unnoticed on the bib of white fur on his chest. Despite himself, he measured the leap. To steal and eat human food . . . His hunger was terrible, but . . . to leap up and tear a dangling ham from its string and rip off a great hunk, and fill his mouth with its marvelous juices and swallow it down . . .

Long strings of drool slowly saturated his bib. The act was a sacrilege. He had stood on a rock rim above a human, the Indian boy, and snarled threateningly. He had actually tried to attack an advancing array of other humans in the strange place where he'd followed the wrong wagon, but that was because those humans were threatening his charges, the mules. To threaten or even bite a human was one crime, but to eat a human's ham . . .

The dog looked away, trembling all over. When he looked up again, it was with profound guilt, and when he slunk out the open door of the kitchen it was a guilty slink. He felt the faintest tinge of pride because he hadn't leaped for the heavenly hams and the glistening sausage, but the pride was very faint. He was burdened with the guilty knowledge that the real reason he hadn't broken the sacred rule was a simple fact—he knew he couldn't reach them.

He felt sure that when the man came, he would be punished. His bobtail sagged despairingly. He limped to the stream and had a long, long drink of water, drinking until he couldn't swallow more, couldn't find room for another drop in his distended belly. It didn't help much, but it was something. He went back to the hayfield to be sure the mules were all right, and as he passed the kitchen he found that he still thought villainously of ham. There was a man-sized boulder near the center of the field. Its side was warm with the sun. He flopped beside it, ignoring the tall grasses which crackled under his matted hide, and stretched himself out against the

149

rock. The comforting scent of the wagon and the mules and the cabin—and the hams—all washed to his nose in the warm, lazy currents of the mountain air. Somewhere within a yard or so he thought he could detect another mouse cache of grass seed. But he just couldn't stop thinking ham. He would wait for the man to come and punish him.

The rock against which he was lying gave him a feeling of protection, and he closed his eyes and fell heavily into sleep, waiting. His muzzle twitched, and his hind legs began to make twitching motions as in his dreams he ran and ran and ran, throughout the rich wildness of his own mountains, and so passed the time until punishment came, waiting.

Sixteen

ANGUS M'TAGGART was sleeping as soundly as a grizzly in winter when the uncle from Louisiana barged in on him near ten o'clock that night in the room M'Taggart sometimes took over his favorite saloon in Durango. He leaped up and nearly knifed the fellow before he awoke enough to be merely hostile instead of homicidal, and he had to put on his boots and get a drink before awakening sufficiently to remember the uncle was a friend and to try to figure out what he was talking about.

Uncle Raleigh had just concluded a late-lasting conversation with one Miss Agatha 'Icks, it appeared, and he'd come with all sorts of gabble and a plan.

The gabble ran to the effect that his nephew was letting this thing about his animals get him down pretty bad. Being the kind of fellow he was, he seemed to figure it was all his fault.

The plan was full of rich complexity, especially for a sleepy man who hadn't thought clearly since they'd gotten back to Durango. It was: distraction over the animals' fate being mandatory, Uncle Raleigh was to allow Nephew Calvin a maximum of a week at his cabin in Salida. Then, if he didn't snap out of the slough of despond, Uncle Raleigh was prepared to bait, push, tempt, and physically haul his nephew all the way to Philadelphia, where some doctor or other was going to give him an operation and make his mouth all well and simultaneously provide no end of distracting activities. Poor Calvin would get over his guilty grief at the loss of the animals, and,

151

not the least of the benefits, he would help himself to a chance at looking and living like a normal man.

M'Taggart thought about it all and nodded and glanced at the bottle again and eventually asked a question: "So why'd you wake me up?"

"Miss Hicks wanted to explain all that," the uncle said. "She's right downstairs."

M'Taggart woke up completely at that. "In a barroom?" he asked incredulously.

"No, of course not. She's waiting outside in her carriage. Maybe you want to wash your face a little? Tuck in your shirt-tails?"

M'Taggart didn't, but he did. He didn't remember quite how long it had been since they'd returned to Durango and he had reported to the saloon, but he had an idea he might be in pretty rough shape to be talking to a lady. And the way the lady looked at him, leaning through the window of her daddy's Stanhope, confirmed his belief, as did her first words.

"See here, Mr. M'Taggart," she said sharply, "just how long do you intend to go on spreeing? You're ruining your health and your reputation."

"What reputation?" M'Taggart asked stubbornly.

"Your reputation with me."

"What about you, Missy?" he said. "Out late at night in front of a saloon?"

She gave him a measuring look. "I'm beginning to wonder if such things matter, Mr. M'Taggart. Other things have to change, at any rate. You feeling conscience-stricken and drinking. Mr. Fairchild feeling conscience-stricken and mop-ing. Now, I want you to do both him and yourself a favor. Go back with him to Salida, first thing in the morning."

"Can't," M'Taggart said. "We're waiting for the pass to open."

"And you know as well as I that it just may not open until next spring. Nobody even knows how much snow fell on Wolf Creek. Nobody's been up to measure it."

"But what would I do in Salida?"

"You're going to stay in Mr. Fairchild's cabin when Mr. Hillman takes him on to Philadelphia."

"You mean *if*."

"No, I mean *when*. If you'll think a minute you'll realize there's no way he'd go as long as there's a Chinaman's chance those poor animals might yet come straggling home. Of course, that's just graveyard whistling, but there's got to be an end to it. Now, you can prospect over around Mr. Fairchild's cabin as easily as you can around yours, and you can just haul yourself out of that dirty saloon and do it." She leaned farther from the Stanhope's window, peering into M'Taggart's favorite dirty saloon, and added curiously, "By the way, Mr. M'Taggart, why in the world is there a stuffed cat up on that shelf yonder?"

M'Taggart couldn't answer. He was still speechless the next morning when he found himself on a genuine train. He'd last ridden a train from Omaha, Nebraska, to San Francisco in '72, and it scarred his soul to learn how fast the things now ran, on a little bitty track no wider than a sheep path, jerking around corners and down grades like a, well, like a locomotive. The southern reaches of the San Juan Mountains whipped by him in mere hours, and then the train was ringing and clanging and trembling its way into Alamosa. No sooner than he'd got his bearings and managed to gawk at the city sights while changing trains than the new train was panting and champing to roll out again.

M'Taggart called himself a fool for coming. The animals were dead, no doubt about it. Nothing but a robust, mountain-savvy animal could have gotten down from that icy pass, and, as M'Taggart knew, even Margaret the mule had been too slab-sided and travel-weary for the odds to be with her. Poor Calvin staring out the window beside M'Taggart knew it too. M'Taggart could tell from the look on his face and the forced cheer with which he responded to the uncle's insistently cheerful conversation.

Until the train whistled out of Alamosa, M'Taggart himself managed only a tooth-gritted smile at Uncle Raleigh's chatter. But once they were in the central stretches of the San Luis Valley, the speed didn't seem as terrible. The tracks were straight and the valley over eighty miles long. M'Taggart finally got his head on straight and helped the uncle make the conversation and tried to do what he'd set out to do, which was to try to ease the mind of the poor fellow.

In Salida, once they finally got off the train, M'Taggart started feeling almost glad to be there. Not that the little railroad town of Salida amounted to anything, and not that Calvin's mountains amounted to much. Oh, admittedly the Sawach Range supposedly had more high peaks than any other range in the Rockies, but to M'Taggart's eyes they didn't look half so grand as his own La Platas and San Juans. But it was a beautiful Indian summer evening, and golden aspen leaves fluttered onto their hats and shoulders after they dropped off an empty ore wagon that had given them a ride back up into the hills, and there was a feeling of sweet solitude that M'Taggart's own mountains sometimes seemed to lack. Around Durango, it was getting so you could hardly walk twenty miles anymore without stumbling over some prospector or tourist or consumptive out living in a tent and trying to cure his lungs with mountain air. And here was Calvin, living only five or six miles from a town, but once they'd turned up the narrow, overgrown road he said went to his cabin, everything was so tidy and quiet you'd guess his nearest neighbor was fifty miles away. M'Taggart gave idle thought to moving.

"Hunting pretty good around your place?" he asked Calvin.

Calvin grinned. "Not for me," he said. "I try sometimes, but I'm too poor a shot."

"Lots of deer tracks," M'Taggart said. He gestured to the side of the road, where a small, cloven hoof had left a clear

154

imprint. Next to it, a wild rose lifted rosy red leaves to vie with the golden shower of the aspens. Pretty, pretty.

"Calvin's going to shoot all them deer with his camera first thing in the morning," Uncle Raleigh proclaimed. "You and me are going to track them down for him, Mr. M'Taggart, and herd them right under his nose. You game?"

"Count on me," M'Taggart said. "But once Calvin's got his picture, well, I'm quite a hand with venison stew. I guess nobody'll mind if I borrow a rifle and do a little shooting of my own, will they?"

"No, sir," Uncle Raleigh said, "and I'd sure admire to tag along with you. We'll have the stew all cooked by the time Calvin quits messing with his pictures. Deer hang out all the time in a meadow right above the cabin. Drop one there, we won't have so far to carry the meat home."

Like M'Taggart, he began watching for deer tracks. They saw it almost simultaneously—a larger, round hoofprint. The print was made by no deer. It looked too small for horse. M'Taggart opened his mouth, then coughed falsely to cover the gasp of surprise he had been unable to suppress. He shot a warning glance at the uncle, and the uncle nodded almost imperceptibly. Mule? Could it possibly be the mules?

They would not get Calvin stirred up all over again. They would wait and see. But they couldn't resist walking faster, then faster yet, until M'Taggart saw Calvin's pensive gaze wander away from the treetops and light on him in perplexity. He coughed again and said, "Thought I heard water. I sure am feeling thirsty."

"Yes, sir, Calvin's got his own private stream, just two more bends in the road," Uncle Raleigh said. He sounded far too innocent, and Calvin began to gaze around, but, thank God, not down, as if trying to figure out the cause of their sudden hurry.

M'Taggart resolutely raised his eyes from the ground, willing Calvin not to look down. Uncle Raleigh began to blather about sunsets here, something about how they only painted up a cloud or two in the east, since the mountains to the west cut

155

off the sun so early, and M'Taggart stubbed his toe agonizingly on the log bridge over the stream because he refused to look down and therefore didn't watch where he was going.

But the cabin dreamed silently under golden aspens sighing against a sky which slowly darkened toward blue shadow. M'Taggart let out an involuntary sigh of his own.

"Well, now, it don't look like much, but it's home," Calvin said. "Just you wait till we get a fire going and some of my grandmother's ham frying. Say, Uncle Raleigh, you remember seeing a bottle anywhere? Seems like there's a bottle put away too."

He clattered up to a little front porch railed with more pine logs and pulled the latch string, apparently anxious to hurry in and make his guests comfortable. M'Taggart's eyes hungrily swept the aspen leaves lying thick around the cabin. He saw nothing, but Uncle Raleigh suddenly threw his arms around M'Taggart and crushed him in a hug that would have done honor to a grizzly bear. "There's fresh tracks over there by the mule lot!" he whispered wildly into M'Taggart's ear. "It's the mules, I swear it!"

"Where? Where?" M'Taggart whispered back.

Their host reappeared on the porch. "Funny thing," he said. "The back door's wide open. Reckon somebody's been here?"

"Now, Calvin," Uncle Raleigh said. "Now, boy, don't get too excited, but it's just barely possible—"

With a snort and a commotion of hurrying hoofs, a red mule dashed around the corner of the cabin from the mule lot. Upon seeing the three men, he instantly drew himself up haughtily and fixed them with an injured gaze. It was Old Jeb. A second red mule danced past him, then whirled and danced back. But it was the black mule who welcomed them. Margaret, following on Young Jeb's heels, stopped and peered at M'Taggart. Recognition dawned. She whinnied her horselike whinny. Old Jeb may have wanted shelled corn and oats, but Margaret wanted oatmeal.

"Hallelujah!" shouted Uncle Raleigh.

156

"Well, I'll be darned," said Calvin. A wide smile spread over his face. "I'll just be darned. Now, you told me the Jebs had a black mule with them, but whoever would have dreamed they'd have brought her all the way along?"

"We saw their tracks," Uncle Raleigh said. "Back on the road there, but I was afraid to say anything."

"Tracks?" Calvin said. "Did you see a . . . ? Is Nemo . . . ?"

The three mules, milling skittishly, backed toward the corner of the house, and M'Taggart stepped toward them. He reached for Margaret, but she whirled away. There was a thud and the sound of three large bodies colliding against the wall of the cabin, then the mules took off like jackrabbits, stamping for the hayfield.

"There they go again," Uncle Raleigh called. "After them!"

Uncle Raleigh and M'Taggart ran after the mules, leaving Calvin blinking in the twilight. "Did you see any dog tracks?" he called after them.

M'Taggart quickly panted to a halt. The mules were retreating through the tall grass, a swirl of bodies still colliding with one another in mule contrariness. There was no sign of the old dog. M'Taggart's heart was pounding in his ears, and for a moment he heard nothing else. But then it came, a growl of warning followed by fierce barking as an old, feeble, black-and-white dog came limping wildly out of the grass, charging them. It was a weak charge, to be sure, and a staggering charge, but a charge nevertheless as the dog struggled as fast as he could to the defense of the mules.

Uncle Raleigh stopped dead in his tracks a few feet ahead of M'Taggart, and Calvin, running to catch up, soon passed the both of them. Calvin's motion must have looked threatening to the dog, because the limping animal came on, even more furiously. Then the old dog stopped so fast that his hind legs slewed under him, and his head went up to catch the wind

157

and the scent that it carried. A great shudder seemed to start at the dog's nose and run through the tip of his bobtail. Suddenly, his deep barking changed into a shrill yap of recognition.

"Nemo! Nemo!" Calvin cried.

He ran toward the dog, but the dog ran even faster, hobbling, stumbling, to meet him. The old dog hurled himself on Calvin, crying and yelping, and bowled him over.

M'Taggart found it necessary to cough again and again. The dog's face wore a hideous expression, lips curled back, underjaw thrust forward, his own version of a smile, and he seemed to be licking everything in sight. He licked Calvin's hands. He licked Calvin's knees. Sometimes he missed and licked the empty air. It was the dog's only form of embracing. Calvin struggled, trying to hug the old dog and trying to get back to his feet, but the dog knocked him over again in an excess of joy, then danced around him on three legs, suddenly a puppy again, whimpering and licking the man's nose, his mouth, his hair.

At first, the old dog ignored the strangers. He had no time for them. Then he must have caught scent of M'Taggart, for he bounded to him in great leaps and shoved M'Taggart in the chest with his one good forepaw, jumping, then in the same way he jumped Uncle Raleigh, whom he'd never seen before, and then he was all over Calvin again, still crying and licking, while Calvin tried to drag him into his lap to comfort him and try to calm him.

But the dog pulled away abruptly, as if some thought had occurred to him. While Calvin called anxiously to him, the dog backed into the wild hay, then turned and trotted hurriedly after the mules, his progress showing only by movement of the grass. The mules' flight had slowed, and they milled near a big boulder near the center of the field until the dog reached them. There was a hoarse bark, then another bark, then the mules slowly advanced toward the humans.

Old Jeb wouldn't come all the way. His forgiveness for the

man's inexplicable neglect apparently wasn't to be won in an instant, and Young Jeb and Margaret, as always, stayed close behind him. But the old dog couldn't seem to stay away any longer from Calvin, for he limped toward him, wagging his bobtail proudly, saying as clearly as words, "Look at me! Look what I did!"

M'Taggart coughed some more. He seemed to have a fly in his throat and a fog in his eyes, spangled with diamonds. But, then, the uncle was just standing there weeping like a little child. Calvin was having trouble too, he saw, when he tried for speech. Calvin failed the first time, but then he succeeded. "Good boy," he sang. "Good dog. You really did it."

M'Taggart joined in the praise, more of the fog bothering him, and even though Uncle Raleigh choked some, he, too, managed to help them brag on the old dog. "Now will you look at that dawg?" he croaked. "He brought them mules all the way home. All them hundreds of miles. Yes, sir, old fellow, you didn't let anything stop you, did you? Yes, sir!" At each word, the dog's stubby bobtail wagged harder, flailing the air, and when he'd had his due he came to Calvin and leaned against his legs. Calvin kneeled and buried his face into the dog's matted fur.

It was some time before Calvin spoke again. Then he said, "Reckon y'all could collar the mules? Silly things, the Jebs never would answer to their names. But maybe if you could rattle a bucket at them, Uncle Raleigh, they'll let you catch them. Looks like I'd better get old Nemo something to eat. He's . . . he's . . ."

Calvin started coughing just as M'Taggart had, still hugging the dog. M'Taggart could see why. The swelling over the old fellow's eye seemed to have healed up, but both eyes were now discharging. And he looked as if he'd been in a bad fight somewhere, M'Taggart thought as he turned back toward the barn and a bucket. And if the dog had any flesh at all now on his old bones, you couldn't tell it by looking.

M'Taggart tramped off. He figured he'd have to get all three

159

mules in by himself, and he wished it weren't getting so dark, or he'd bring home as much venison as that old dog could eat in a whole new lifetime. He only hoped Calvin had on hand something else to feed him. Oatmeal, preferably. Once he got Margaret and the others rounded up, they'd need plenty of oatmeal.

There was no oatmeal, M'Taggart learned to his dismay a little later, but at least there was plenty of corn and plain oats, and plenty of sausage and ham. Sitting in the kitchen, with the stove popping warmly and the candles lit, he'd had to caution Calvin against giving the old dog too much of the ham at one time. And that sausage, smelling of too much garlic and rather a lot of sage and, he could swear, red hot pepper—why, sausage like that might kill even a young, healthy dog.

But finally the mules were fed and watered and bedded down in clean hay, and finally the dog had stopped gulping ham, and it was time to relax, M'Taggart noted—and ham sizzling for themselves in the skillet, with another skilletful of some of that sausage, which, now that M'Taggart came to think of it, didn't smell so bad.

They sat in the kitchen.

"Nephew, raise the lid on that Dutch oven. That biscuit is smelling pretty near done to me."

M'Taggart thought the biscuits could use another five or ten minutes, but he was feeling comfortable and tired, so he didn't bother saying so. He was watching the old dog, and the dog was watching Calvin as if he were afraid to take his eyes off him. But as M'Taggart sipped slowly, he saw the dog glance away from Calvin and into a dark corner on the other side of the stove.

"Get some sleep, old fellow," he urged.

"He needs it," Calvin said, reaching down to scratch the dog's ears.

160

"A long, long sleep," Uncle Raleigh agreed comfortably. Calvin looked uneasy. "Well, not too long."

Uncle reassured nephew, and M'Taggart began to smile as the old dog circled, circled, worn toenails clicking faintly on the wooden floor. He settled himself in the corner by the stove with a groan so exactly like a weary man's that they all three laughed.

The dog opened his mouth in his grin and laughed with them. In a moment or two the chin sank, and then it was on the floor. The rheumy eyes closed.

M'Taggart couldn't help it. He held his breath and watched the old dog anxiously. From the corner of his eye he saw that Calvin was also watching anxiously, and M'Taggart forced himself to laugh and say, "Looks like he's all in."

At the sound of M'Taggart's voice, the dog started awake and looked around wildly, worriedly.

"Now, now," Calvin said soothingly. "Everything's all right. Go back to sleep."

But the dog apparently decided not to stay by the stove. Toenails clicked again and the dog padded over to Calvin and put his head on Calvin's knee. He seemed to wait until the immediately forthcoming hand found just the right spot under his ragged ears, and then the eyes closed and the body relaxed against the knee of Calvin, his master, the one man.

"Now that's a right peaceful sight," Uncle Raleigh said.

With the dog out in the candlelight, M'Taggart could see him more clearly, and he saw that the matted sides swelled in and out with the dog's regular breathing.

M'Taggart began to feel good. He sipped again and thought about tomorrow. He didn't know what this Calvin Fairchild was going to do about some doctor in Philadelphia, when his animals so obviously needed a long, long spell of staying at home. He didn't know what this Raleigh Hillman was going to do about going home to Louisiana, when he'd obviously fallen in love with the real country, the mountains. He hadn't the slightest idea what Miss Agatha 'Icks was going to do when she got the telegram Calvin swore he was going to send in by Uncle Raleigh tomorrow.

But M'Taggart had a pretty good idea what he would do. Of course, humans acting the way they did, there was always the possibility Calvin would want to keep all three mules, but just to be on the safe side and see that Margaret's attachment to him remained unmistakable, M'Taggart decided he'd stroll the five or six miles into Salida with the uncle in the morning and pick up a fifty-pound sack of oatmeal.